THE ASSISTANT

John Tristan

A NineStar Press Publication

www.ninestarpress.com

The Assistant

Printed in the USA

Print ISBN: 978-1-64890-073-0

First Edition, August, 2020

Also available in eBook, ISBN: 978-1-64890-072-3

WARNING:

This book contains sexually explicit content, which is only suitable for mature readers, discussion of depression, dealing with a chronic illness/disability, depiction of a D/s relationship between boss and employee, and a heavy caning scene.

Burned out ex-soldier Nick Kurosawa has drifted from job to job since he lost his family in a car crash. Lately, he's been working on and off as a bouncer, barely managing to cover his bills; an opportunity for steady, well-paying work is just what he needs to get his life back in order.

Jacob Umber, a secretive philanthropist, gives him that opportunity. Umber has fibromyalgia and needs a personal assistant to help him with the tasks of daily living—someone strong, adaptable, and, most of all, willing to let Umber take the lead.

It seems a perfect opportunity for Nick. More than anything, he craves guidance and a purpose, and Umber gives him that in spades. When Nick starts craving more, it seems an impossible complication, but even the reserved Umber can't deny Nick's talent—and need—for following his orders. But Umber's shadowy past holds secrets that could undo their fragile new relationship and any hope Nick has of a normal life.

To my chosen family—thank you for everything.

Part One

MEETINGS

It was a clear autumn night, with the moon low and yellow above the city. Between its fullness and the lights, only a few stars could be made out, pinpoints in the raw black silk of the night. Nick stood with his fists balled above the man breathing hard in the gutter. A trickle of spilled beer ran into his hair, foaming like shampoo. He smelled sour, of sweat and fear.

"Jesus, man!" The man's companion—a skinny young guy with a circular Band-Aid over one eye, like a discount pirate—crouched beside him. "Somebody call an ambulance! Call the cops!"

"By all means," Nick said. He forced himself to take a step back, unclench his fists. "Let's call the cops and tell them the whole story."

Discount Pirate slit his eye at him and helped his companion to his feet. The man was dazed but seemed unhurt. Still—he could easily have a concussion.

Nick hesitated. "Maybe we should call an ambulance—"

"Forget it," the man said thickly and spat into the gutter. In the neon and moonlight, the blood in his mouth looked black. His eyes met Nick's, and this was the worst part: they understood each other perfectly. He'd wanted to start a fight, and Nick had taken the bait. Another night, it would have fallen out differently.

"Let's get out of here," Discount Pirate said, putting a proprietary arm around his companion's waist and dragging him off into the darkness.

Nick let out a shaky breath. The street was empty, now; if he was lucky, this wouldn't get back to Merritt, who owned the Hellhole. He hadn't hired Nick to start fights but to stop them as gently as possible—de-escalation, not macho bullshit. The Hellhole was the only gay bar in Westerley, which meant it drew both the occasional snickering asshole and its share of ex-boyfriend drama. Merrick wouldn't thank him for bad publicity.

"Jesus, Nick."

Fuck. This was the last thing he needed. He turned toward the familiar voice. "Hey, Alex."

Alexander Finn—his friend, once-upon-a-time fuck-buddy, and self-appointed social worker—had come up out of the Hellhole at just the wrong time. Sweat was still beaded on his pale forehead, cooling rapidly in the night air. "What happened?"

"Didn't know you were down here tonight," Nick said, affecting a breezy tone. "Must have been here before my shift started."

Alex rolled his eyes. "I know you're not jealous, so you're trying to deflect. What happened?" He took out his cigarette case—silver, engraved—and popped one into his bow-lipped mouth, then offered one to Nick.

He reached for it, then hesitated. "Haven't smoked in months."

Alex gave him a skeptical look. "Come on."

"Vaping doesn't count."

He laughed softly. "I'll give you that one." He snapped the case closed and tucked it away. "Talk."

"I don't know." Nick ran his hands through his hair. "The guy just. Got under my skin. It's like he knew how to push my buttons."

"You're not supposed to have buttons while you're on the door."

"Fuck you. Give me a cigarette."

He did; they smoked together in the neon-lit dark.

"This job..." Alex chewed on his thoughts for a moment. "It's not good for you. This isn't the first time you've let someone...push your buttons."

Alex was right—he'd never let himself take it this far before, but there were more than a few times over the last few weeks when a sneer or a snicker or a muttered insult had gotten under his skin and launched him right in someone's face, teeth bared, eyes glittering. His fuse frayed shorter every week he was out here. He took a long, slow draw from the cigarette and laughed bitterly. "Well. I still need the rent paid."

"How long until your shift is over?"

Nick grinned sideways at Alex. "Why, you want to take me home?"

He sighed and shook his head, but it had raised a smile. "Just think you could do with a good night's sleep. After that..." Alex hesitated a moment. "Can you take the next few days off?"

"I'm not back on shift until Monday evening."

Alex nodded and took a card out of his pocket—his business card, Nick recognized—and then fished out a pen. "Turn around," he said.

Nick did. Alex leaned on him, using his back as a desk to write on. He could feel the scratch of the pen through his shirt.

When Alex was done, he handed him the card. Nick frowned at it. There was an address on it, a place in the financial district, and a name: Jacob Umber. "What's this?"

"Someone—someone I know is looking to hire. I thought...well, you already have a job, and I had someone else lined up, but—"

"You always have someone lined up for something, don't you?" There was a slight edge of bitterness to Nick's words. Alex networked—he always had a side hustle lined up for someone, for the washouts and burnouts, the ex-cops and ex-military, the bikers and drifters he seemed to draw into his orbit. His type: like Nick. "Is this meant to be charity? Because you can pass it on to one of your other tricks. I don't need it."

"Call it what you will. And you're not a trick, Nicholas." Alex leaned in to kiss him on the cheek, chastely. "You're my friend."

Nick swallowed a sudden lump in his throat and stuffed the card in the back pocket of his jeans. "Yeah, all right, fine. There's no number on the card—am I meant to just show up?"

"I wrote hours on there," Alex said. "Nine to three. Weekdays."

"Right."

"Nick..." He seemed to be struggling with his words. "This isn't a guaranteed job. I can get you a way in, but you'll have to impress."

"Come on, Alex." Nick flashed a smile. "Don't you think I can pull out the stops when I need to?"

He laughed and shook his head. "I know you can. Good luck, Nick."

"Thanks. No, really...thank you."

He nodded and left him on the empty street. Nick took his vape out of his pocket and sucked down a nicotine cloud; he noticed his hands were shaking. There was a subtle ache in his knuckles, where they'd collided with the man's cheekbone. He felt a tiredness deeper than exhaustion, something like lead in his bones, and on top of that, a thin hot skin of queasy arousal. He didn't know if he wanted to sleep for a year or get fucked up against the wall of the nearest alley. Well, he told himself, right now it's going to be neither. He smoked until his hands stopped shaking and then waited for the sky to lighten—for his shift to be over—so he could go home.

*

Nick woke up after four hours of sleep, with the sun noon-high and streaming through his thin curtains. It gave his apartment an almost cinematic look, gauzy and warm. Then a cloud passed over the sun, and the apartment looked like what it actually was—half a step up from a shitty motel, with peeling wallpaper and mismatched furniture.

He got up, showered, and bothered to shave too. The face that looked back from his small bathroom mirror seemed suddenly younger, if equally tired. You'll have to impress, Alex had said, but even with his best suit on, Nick didn't see anything too impressive. A low-ranking yakuza in a bad action movie, maybe.

He snorted to himself and shook his head. It'd have to do. He made himself a strong, sweet coffee and called it breakfast, then went on his way.

The address on the card was in the financial district, but past the banks and high-rise offices, in an older part of the city. The buildings had the look of being grand, once upon a time, but were now slightly faded and ragged around the edges, the facades gray with ages of dirt. Most of them seemed to be houses, but every now and then, Nick spotted a discreet plaque near the doors: law firms, accountants, and other, vaguer businesses. One, with a leering gargoyle over the door, was a "wealth consultant."

Nick expected he would find Jacob Umber in one of those offices. When he reached his destination, though, he realized it was actually either a store, or the display of someone's collection of knick-knacks. The place was small, glass-fronted, the windows crammed with what looked to him to be various antiques and curiosities. There was an ancient pistol, a carved wooden idol, a set of scrimshaw. The card Alex had given him seemed to burn in his fingers. Most likely, it was just that he'd been rubbing it, again and again, between his thumb and first two fingers, thinning the paper to a silky texture. He tucked it in his pocket—no need for it anymore—and went inside.

There was no name or sign on the door, but a small sign proclaimed the same hours Alex had written on the card, handwritten in jade-green ink. A bell over the door jangled atonally. Nick had the instant sensation of being watched, though he saw nobody, only a shadowy depth of shelves and bric-a-brac, crowded to the ceiling. Hanging from the ceiling, in a few cases. A cow skull leered at him eyelessly. A curved silver sword hung suspended in sisal. A brown trunk, tucked in a hammock of crossed leather straps.

At first sight, the shop looked empty, an abandoned warren. Even when he turned the corner and came face to face with the desk, Nick didn't see anyone for a moment. Then the shadows shifted, ever so slightly, and he saw him—a man in a high-backed chair just beside the desk, watching him.

He seemed...average, at a first glance. White, probably, and neither small nor large, forty-something, indistinct brownish hair. But there was something about him, some poised alertness, that raised gooseflesh on the back of Nick's neck.

Nick cleared his throat. "Sorry to bother you. I'm looking for Jacob Umber?"

"I am Mr. Umber," the man corrected. He wore a gray worsted suit with a plain black tie, and well-polished black Oxfords. One knee was fixed in a hinged, carbon-black brace.

Nick raised his eyebrows. This one was a stickler for formal manners. "My apologies. Mr. Umber. My name is Nick Kurosawa. Alexander Finn said you might have work for me?"

Some flicker of expression passed over Umber's impassive features. "I know. Mr. Finn passed on your details."

Nick had never heard Alex referred to as Mr. Finn before.

Umber rose from his chair, his knee giving him a moment's difficulty. He was shorter than he seemed sitting down—just about a head shorter than Nick—but broader, too, with unexpected muscle beneath the neat lines of his suit jacket. He looked Nick up and down with clinical interest. His eyes were gray bordering on green. For a brief, wild moment as Umber approached him, Nick wondered if Alex had sent him here to be pimped out, but Umber's flat, assessing look wiped out any thought of that possibility.

"I assume you're hiring for close-protection work?" It was a guess, but Nick's instincts weren't usually off base. Umber somehow had the air of a man who got into trouble.

Umber smiled. It had an odd effect on his face, not quite a pleasant one. "I'm actually looking for something more...all-round."

Fuck. Maybe Alex *had* pimped him out. Nick shifted from foot to foot. There was something unsettling about Umber's flat regard—something that made the tips of Nick's ears burn. "All-round," he echoed, trying for a tone as flat as Umber's.

"I am looking to hire a personal assistant."

Nick blinked. "You mean a secretary?"

"I may need my PA to make appointments for me occasionally, but, no." He sighed and tapped his knee brace. "This was a bad fall, but I fell because of muscle fatigue. I have fibromyalgia—do you know what that is?"

Nick had a vague idea. "A chronic illness?"

Again, that unsettling smile played over Umber's face. "Yes. Chronic and variable. It means that some days I'm fine, and some days I can barely manage to get out of bed.

"And...this would include occasional close-protection work?"

Umber held his gaze, the smile dropping away and leaving his face as flat and neutral as before. "You would be fully briefed, should I decide you're right for the job. And if you decide to take it."

Nick had the sudden urge to stand at attention. He fought it down, internally squirming under Umber's eyes. "I'll be honest, I've never worked as a personal assistant. I don't know much about helping disabled people."

"I don't want someone trained to 'help disabled people,'" Umber said, with a faint hint of distaste around the words. "I want someone without preconceived notions—someone adaptable, who takes instruction easily."

Nick raised his eyebrows. "Well. That I can do."

"We shall see." There was a thread of humor in Umber's voice now, cool and razor-thin. "Do you have references besides Mr. Finn?"

There weren't many, but Nick had come prepared, here, at least—a letter from his old CO and from his last close-protection job. Nothing from Merritt, yet. Umber sat back down—this time in a chair by an old-fashioned desk—and read through them, quickly but thoroughly. Usually Nick hated watching someone read his reference letters, but it was almost a relief having Umber's assessing eyes off of him.

"Thank you, Mr. Kurosawa," he said after a minute or two. "Do you mind if I keep these?"

"No, go ahead. They're copies."

Umber nodded and put them away in one of the desk drawers. "And do you have a résumé with you as well?"

He didn't bother reading through that, but put it facedown on top of the desk after giving it a cursory glance. If having the Hellhole on his résumé was a deal-breaker for him, he didn't seem to show it—not that Nick thought it would be if Alex recommended him for the job. There was an awkward moment—or at least, it seemed awkward to Nick—where they were both silent. Then Nick cleared his throat, just to fill the emptiness with some kind of noise.

Umber looked up. "That's all. I'll be in touch."

Nick took a breath and restrained his first impulse. What that was, he wasn't sure, but there was something about Umber's response that needled him, and he knew he wasn't rational when he was needled. He nodded. "Thank you, Mr. Umber."

"You're welcome."

God, had the man trained to keep his voice that flat and expressionless?

Nick turned around—there was no temptation to mill around Umber's strange little store—and headed out the door. Once in the open air, he took a few shaky breaths. He realized his heart had been hammering at double speed for the last five minutes, at least. He glanced at his phone. He'd been in there for ten minutes total. It felt like more. It felt exhausting.

Some impulse spurred him to take out his wallet and slide the picture from behind his driver's license—him and Lily, the last time they'd been photographed together. She'd been a toddler, and he'd been in uniform. They were smiling in the sun. Their mom had taken the picture. She's been so proud, their mom, and Lily starstruck by his khaki. It was a mercy they never saw him slide off the rails of his promising military career and into...well. Into taking whatever hustles his fuck-buddy managed to slide his way.

That's not true. He made himself think it. This job could be something, a real opportunity. Alex might have gotten him through the door, but it was up to him to make something of it.

If Umber chose him, that was.

*

He didn't hear from Umber the next day, nor the day after that. By the time Monday rolled around, he'd given up on the idea and picked up double shifts at the Hellhole in order to make the rent. It'd be tight, and he'd have to live on ramen a few days, but it was doable.

He hadn't heard from Alex either. Nick figured that the other person Alex had had in mind had gotten the job. He wished them well. It was probably for the best. Nick wasn't the sort to wipe anyone's ass, really, or help them cross the street. He was better off here, glowering with crossed arms in front of the Hellhole's door, spooking off crowds of curious college boys who'd had a few too many drinks.

He sighed and put his hands on his hips. The door behind him opened, and a few of the Hellhole's late-night clients spilled out onto the streets, oblivious to his presence. He'd become a part of the scenery to them. He watched them go, tracking their trail down the street, watching their loose, giggly camaraderie become quiet caution the farther they got from the Hellhole's sanctuary.

"Mr. Kurosawa."

He blinked and turned around. Nobody called him that here, not even his boss. There was a cold, dry moment of fear—almost panic—in which he ran through every one of the worst possibilities: a cop come to arrest him, Discount Pirate's belligerent buddy dead after a brain aneurysm.

It wasn't a cop, or anyone bearing terrible news. Half a second after he turned, his brain caught up with the rest of him, and he recognized the voice before he saw the man's face: Jacob Umber, of the mysterious store and the mysterious job.

He was just as well-dressed as he'd been when Nick had met him, except he'd added the slight ornamentation of a hunter-green necktie and leaned on a silver-tipped cane. There was something slightly obnoxious about how well-put-together he looked at, what, four AM? There didn't seem to be a single hair out of place.

He'd been prepared for some sarcastic rejoinder to come to mind, some biting comment about the job, or how the Hellhole didn't seem like Jacob Umber's usual haunt, but nothing came. Instead, he inclined his head and said "Mr. Umber."

"Quiet night?" Umber's face was just on the edge of impassive, not disinterested, just...polite.

Nick raised his eyebrows. "Quiet enough. What brings you here?"

"The same thing, I suppose, that brings most of your clientele."

He huffed a laugh. "They're not my clientele."

Umber inclined his head, as if to say fair enough. "The establishment's, then."

It was faintly amusing how he somehow managed to avoid saying "the Hellhole." Nick had to admit it was kind of an embarrassing name. There was a moment's silence between them, punctuated only by the sound of a distant siren.

Nick cleared his throat. "By the way, thank you for—for the job interview. Giving me a chance, I mean—"

"I haven't made a decision yet."

It was said in a mild tone, but it threw Nick off-balance. They'd met on his turf, but suddenly the power had shifted, and it was like being back on the mat, trying to make a good impression.

Nick took a long, slow breath. Fuck that. He wasn't on interview manners now. "Lots of candidates to choose from?"

If Umber noticed the sarcasm, he didn't give a sign. "A few."

Nick shifted slightly, shoulders squaring. "I notice you're no longer wearing your brace."

"No," Umber said. "The cane suffices, for now."

More silence spread between them like fog, but Umber made no move to leave. Nick's heartbeat was palpable in the hollow of his throat, and his lips were dry; he resisted the urge to lick them. Was he attracted to Umber? No—that couldn't be it. The man wasn't his type at all. But one thing was true: Umber unsettled him in a way Nick couldn't quite put his finger on. Perhaps it was how in control he looked when at any given moment, Nick's life was spinning out into chaos.

"You're bored here, aren't you?"

It could have sounded offensive, but somehow Umber managed to make it sound nothing save... interested. As if it actually mattered to him that Nick was, in fact, bored out of his skull doing doorman work for the Hellhole.

Nick took a long look at the shorter man. In the dim city lights his eyes seemed black—he was entirely monochrome, save for the green of his tie, made lurid by occasional flashes of neon.

"Yes," he finally said. Why not go for honesty? "But it pays the bills."

Umber nodded. "We're all constrained by our debts, one way or another."

Somehow I doubt you know what it's like to be constrained by debts. Not that Nick would say it. That was too much honesty, probably. Still, the suit, the store in the financial district, even the way Umber carried himself—that irreducible confidence—all spoke to a life of privilege Nick had never even scraped the bottom of.

Two men emerged from the club. One of them body-checked Nick on his way out, then looked back, hazily apologetic, a tipsy smile showing through a bushy black beard. Nick's eyes narrowed—it was oddly as if something important had been interrupted—but the man's conciliatory smile took the edge off his irritation. "Sorry," the man said.

"No problem." Nick nodded to him.

When he turned back, Umber was making his way down the street, back turned to Nick, the click of his cane and his shoes a slightly jagged rhythm. Nick thought about calling after him but dismissed the idea after about half a second's contemplation. Let him pull his man-of-mystery act. Nick didn't have time for those kinds of games when he was on the clock. He folded his arms again and leaned up against the doorjamb.

His shift finished the way it started: quiet, ordinary, dull. He clocked out on his phone—thank God for technology. Ever since Merritt had switched to an app for managing his doormen, Nick hadn't even needed to see him, or anyone inside the club. On nights like tonight, that suited him just fine.

He was about to head home when he heard a voice behind him, half-familiar. He turned and found himself face to face with the man who'd collided with him earlier. Nick looked him up and down, from booted feet to grinning, bearded face. He met the grin with an answering smile, half-sided and almost cynical. "Did you hang around until I got off shift?"

The man shrugged. "Went for a drink at a friend's and decided to wander back, see if you were still there."

"Well." This man was Nick's type, or at least the promise of it: big belly, big biceps, big rough hands, bright eyes sparkling with a mischief that could turn malign at any moment. "I'm still here."

"Come home with me," the man said, and there was no question mark in his sentence. The skin on the back of Nick's neck prickled. God, it had been a while, hadn't it?

"Gonna tell me your name, first?"

The man smirked and dropped his voice low. "Call me Sir."

Nick half laughed. Any other night, he'd probably have told Sir to go fuck himself, never mind the bulging biceps, but he was still...unsettled. Not to mention horny. "All right," he said, "if that's how you want to play it, Sir."

*

When they reached Sir's apartment and he told him to kneel the moment the door closed behind them, Nick was expecting it. He pawed at the man's crotch, going for the zipper, but was rewarded only by a meaty hand in his hair, pulling his head back at a painful angle.

"Uh-uh," he said. "Bad boy."

Nick hissed between his teeth, half not wanting to play the game—just wanting to get fucked. Something in the man's eyes stopped him, though, and he watched, silent. Sir looked down at him, a pleased smile fixed on his face.

"Stay," he said, and released his hair.

Nick stayed.

The man vanished into the back for a moment. Nick remained on his knees, breathing a little raggedly. He was half-hard, a little anxious, a little…bored? He fought down a snicker. *Really, Kurosawa, how jaded are you, exactly?*

The boredom fell away the next moment when the man returned with a collar.

"Hey," Nick said hoarsely, "I don't think—"

"Then don't," the man said with flat precision. "Don't think."

The world seemed to slide away from him then. He let Sir put the collar on him, his heart beating against it until he thought his veins would pop. The moment seemed to stretch and warp, the room swimming as if he were drunk.

Then it was over—ordinary time resumed, and the man's grin was suddenly almost goofy. "Good boy," he said. "Now strip! That's it. Do it slowly."

Something in his tone was…not quite off-putting, but not right either. Why couldn't he have kept talking in that soft, precise way? Not this porno dialog. Nick struggled out of his clothes—he'd never been one for putting on a show—but Sir didn't seem to notice his lack of elegance.

"There you go," he said, rubbing his hardening cock through his jeans. "Uh-huh."

When Nick was naked, he looked up at Sir, the collar suddenly heavy and unnatural around his neck. "Now wh—"

"Shh, puppy, hush up."

Puppy? Nick couldn't help a sarcastic eyebrow raise—but again, Sir didn't seem to notice, or care.

"Hands and knees, boy."

He dropped to his hands and knees, obedient enough. His cock was still half-hard, and he hoped Sir would know how to get it to full mast.

Sir circled him appreciatively, then said, "Stay," again, drawing out the vowels with cloying condescension.

Nick closed his eyes and counted aloud. By the time he'd reached forty, Sir was back, and he'd lost his hard-on entirely.

A slick, gloved hand probing his hole with well-practiced care managed to get him hard again, and quick. It almost felt like cheating to Nick, but he wasn't going to look a gift horse in the mouth. Sir fucked his hole first with two fingers, then three, pushing up against the sensitive spot inside him until his cock was leaking and jumping against his belly. Then he withdrew his hand, and something else—something thick and solid—entered Nick's ass. Not the man's cock: this was cold, and too hard. He craned his neck to look behind him.

Protruding from his ass was a curved, black dog's tail.

"That's right," Sir said with the same big, shit-eating grin, "wag your little tail, puppy."

Nick breathed out sharply and pulled away. With one movement, he pulled the plug out of his ass and stood up. "We're done here."

"Hey, I—"

"You don't fucking spring that shit on someone without talking about it first. We're done."

Sir held up his hands. "Sorry. You seemed into it when I called you puppy, so I thought—"

Nick closed his eyes and counted to five, unfastening the collar which had suddenly become horribly constricting around his neck. "Words and fucking tail plugs aren't the same thing."

"Yeah, shit, I'm sorry." Sir rubbed the back of his neck. "My bad, all right?"

All the man's authority seemed to have left him, and suddenly Nick kind of felt bad for him. "Look, I'll just...go to the bathroom and get an Uber. No harm, no foul."

"You can stay if you want," Sir said. "You don't have to do anything. Hey, crash on the couch; I can make you breakfast."

Nick shook his head. "No, thanks."

There was a moment's silence while Nick pulled on his clothes.

"My name's Gordon," the man said after a while.

"I'm Nick."

"I, uh." He rubbed the back of his head, looking sheepish. "I usually have better instincts about this."

Nick almost smiled. "We all strike out sometimes."

"Guess so." He pointed down the hallway. "Bathroom is second door on the left. Use the yellow towel; it's freshly washed."

"Thanks."

In the bathroom, Nick went to the toilet and cleaned himself up, then washed his hands and face in steaming, soapy water. He looked at his face in the mirror, bags under his eyes, hair in wet disarray. *You're a mess, Kurosawa.* He grunted and dried himself off with the fresh yellow towel, then walked back into the living room.

Gordon had tidied away all the accoutrements of sex, the lube and the collar and that plug. He'd pulled off the leather shirt he was wearing before, too, and had replaced it with a white cotton T-shirt. When he saw Nick come in, he gave a wan smile. "You all right? Still want to get that Uber? I'll pay."

Nick was absurdly moved by the gesture. "Hey, no, you don't have to—"

"No, I insist," he said, smiling faintly, and Nick let him insist. It wasn't as if he had money to spare on gestures.

When the car was ordered, Gordon went into the kitchen and returned with two glasses of water. Nick took his gratefully, drinking it down in three long gulps. He hadn't realized until then how thirsty he was.

"Look," Gordon said after a while, "I, uh, know I got the specifics wrong, but..."

Nick was about to say something, and Gordon must have read it in his face.

"I'm not trying to hit on you again," he said, "but Westerley isn't exactly the biggest pond if you're gay and kinky. So, here, I'd like you to have this." He slid his wallet out of his back pocket and took out a black business card.

Nick took it. It shone like an oil slick under the lights, a subtle, sinister rainbow; whoever had designed it had done a damn good job. There was an address that Nick didn't recognize, embossed in tasteful matte black on the shining dark rainbow.

"Last Friday of the month," Gordon said. "They won't let you in without one of those cards, so don't lose it."

"Sounds mysterious," Nick deadpanned.

Gordon shrugged. "The guys that run this place prefer to keep things discreet."

"Fair enough." Nick tucked the card away. "Thanks. I mean that. I might not ever show up, but...good to have the opportunity."

"You're a straightforward guy, Nick." He grinned lopsidedly. "I like that a lot. You don't see it often enough."

Nick lifted one shoulder in a half shrug. "Life's too short not to be honest with people."

Gordon's smile was almost sad. "I wish there were more people who thought like you."

*

The sun was rising by the time Nick was on the way home, painting the sky in tones of amber and violet. He wasn't so much tired as beyond tiredness—he felt unreal in his own skin. A kind of white noise filled his head, blurring away all coherent thoughts. He watched the city streets roll by, touched by violet-gold light, and nowhere seemed familiar to him.

He somehow made it home and into bed without bothering to take off more than his shoes. When he woke up a few hours later, he realized he'd not even taken off his belt. A second later, he realized why he was awake. His phone was ringing, vibrating madly in his pocket. He groped for it; it read Private Number and the time. Eight thirty AM.

Fuck. He cleared his throat a few times and hit answer. "Hello?" His voice was passably human, at least.

"Mr. Kurosawa. This is Jacob Umber."

There were a few horrible seconds when he had no idea who Jacob Umber was—where he barely had an idea who Mr. Kurosawa was. Then consciousness snapped back to him, and he sat upright in bed. "Mr. Umber. How can I help?"

"I've decided, provisionally, to offer you the job."

He took a deep breath. "Thank you. Uh. Provisionally, meaning...?"

"Your references were satisfactory. Because of the nature of the work of a PA, though, I would prefer a provisional period before anything formal is put in place. After you are walked through an average day, you might decide it isn't for you, and I might decide the—" There was a small pause while he searched for the word. "The fit just isn't right. However, I am optimistic."

"That's great." *Would be even better if my head didn't feel full of cotton wool.* "When should I—"

"Would this afternoon work for you?"

He was meant to be off tonight, but he had planned to spend the day recovering from last night. Still, despite Umber's reassurances that he would "work with him" on making his shifts line up, Nick had an instinct that it was better not to keep him waiting. Call it making a good impression on the new boss. "Absolutely," he said, swallowing back the gravel in his throat. "I can be there in an hour."

"That won't be necessary." Nick swore there was a thread of cool amusement in Umber's voice. "Three o'clock will be more than sufficient. That is when I close up shop and head home. Meet me there—quarter to three, if you'd like to be early."

"I'll be there."

"Excellent. Goodbye, Mr. Kurosawa."

"Good—" Nick started saying, but Umber had already hung up, leaving him talking to an empty line.

He sighed and got out of bed. Sleeping in his clothes and under the covers had left him unpleasantly sweaty. His underwear had cut into his waist uncomfortably, and he smelled...well, rank. A shower and a change were definitely needed before he went and faced Jacob Umber.

He let the hot water run down his body a little too long after he'd rinsed off the last of the soap, luxuriating in the feeling of it. His dingy stall of a shower wasn't much of a spa, but it did for the moment. The gluey, awful feeling of having slept in last night's clothes vanished bit by bit with every drop of water, sluicing away the smell and the awkwardness of it.

God. He never should have gone home with Gordon in the first place. Types like that never ended well for him. He had better luck with...well, with people like Alex, people whose desires were pretty uncomplicated. In the end, he supposed Gordon's desires were pretty uncomplicated, too—a puppy to wag their tail for him—but there was less chance of crossed wires when you stuck with the more vanilla end.

Nick closed his eyes and let the water run over him, thrumming against his forehead. He kept seeing Gordon's grin in his mind's eye. That and the stupid little tail plug, like the punctuation mark on a mistake. Why did he keep gravitating to these men? He liked men who took control, men who could make him hold still while they hurt him. Why did it always end up being guys who wanted things that he couldn't give, that he couldn't be: someone to wrap in rubber, someone to call them master or daddy, someone to wear a tail.

It wasn't that he thought any of those things were wrong, or even particularly off-putting. It was just that they bored him, snapped him out of the moment. Brought him back to earth when he should have been soaring.

He kept gravitating back to it though. The rubber, puppy, master-daddy-sir stuff bored him, but the vanilla stuff bored him too. The truth was that Nick had never found sex very interesting—sure, he got horny, and getting off felt nice, but that feeling of something charged in his fingertips, of an engine thrumming in his belly? That had come twice or three times in his life, every time when someone had been hurting him. A hard caning, once. A drunken hookup that had smirked at him and slapped his face while riding his dick. A few more times that slipped his sleep-deprived mind.

He turned the water to freezing cold for a moment and stood there, shivering, until he was about as awake as he was going to get, then turned it off and stepped out of the shower.

Nick threw on something slightly more casual than what he'd worn to the "interview" and headed out. There was something depressing about staying in his little apartment when everyone else was out at work. It was part of what working the night shift did to you, but usually he'd be sleeping through the day. Once Umber had called, there was no chance of him getting back to sleep. Even though he more than suspected the man knew his schedule, and expected him to nap some more before coming. Nick snorted. In that case, it would have been nice to call at noon, instead of during normal-person hours.

Westerley might not have been the most exciting city in the world, but there was enough to keep someone occupied even on a Monday morning, even someone as financially challenged as Nick. He went to the central library, a beautiful building in the oldest part of town, all white facade and massive wooden doors.

He bought a cheap coffee from the vending machine and made his way over to one of the reading tables, settling in with a sigh and wrapping his autumn-cold fingers around the cardboard cup to warm them. Some magazines were spread out on the table, and by the time he'd discarded the *National Geographic*s and the *Times* and was working his way through the *Westerley Whisperer,* he knew he was bored. Still, he kept flipping the pages with a kind of dogged persistence, as if the stack of magazines was a stack of homework he had to get through. Maybe it was just the idea that if he stopped, he'd have to walk back out into the city, have to think of something else to do.

He turned another page. There was an article about a city councillor who wanted to pass a resolution making Westerley a sanctuary city. There were a few quotes, most of them against the idea. One of the few who seemed for it was a startlingly familiar name.

Local businessman Jacob Umber said: "There are few things I could think of that would be better for Westerley, both as a matter of principle and as a matter of pride. I wholeheartedly endorse this resolution."

It certainly sounded like him. The word choices, the slightly finicky way of talking. Nick could almost imagine how he'd said it, not exactly with passion but with a kind of quiet emphasis that held its own weight.

He closed the magazine. Struck by a sudden inspiration, he went to one of the library's search terminals and typed in "Jacob Umber."

There was an online copy of the article in the *Westerley Whisperer*, and a record of him as the owner of Eight Street Curiosities—the store, even though no sign with that name was seen anywhere near it. At least it was on Eight Street. Nothing else, at least nothing that was indexed. A little more digging showed him that up until a year ago, Eight Street Curiosities had belonged to a woman named Margaret Mason. Now, *she* had plenty of records associated with her name. "Maggie" Mason been a patron of the library, a beloved cornerstone of the community, active in local politics. Her obituary said she'd died after a short illness at the age of eighty-three, with no surviving relatives.

He wondered if the store had gone to auction, then— if that was how Umber picked it up. It surprised him a little; it had had the feel of something long-curated, something with the weight of history behind it. He'd somehow imagined that Umber had picked out all the pieces himself. Nick had even made up stories behind them, he realized: maybe Umber had found the old trunk in a warehouse, the skull at an auction. *Hell of an imagination.* He shook his head, grinning. So what if he'd bought it off some dead old woman? It was his store now.

Nick glanced at his phone. Two o'clock—time had flown. How long had he spent combing through the records for mention of Jacob Umber? And after all that, he wasn't even listed in the Westerley phone book.

Nick got up, his stomach turning slightly. Part of it was hunger—he'd forgotten all about lunch—and part of it was nerves. First day on the job nerves, he guessed, even though it wasn't even properly his first day.

Nothing to do except face it and make his way to Umber's shop.

*

The door was unlocked; Umber sat at his desk, writing a letter with a fountain pen. He hadn't seemed to notice when Nick came in, so Nick cleared his throat.

Umber looked up and smiled abstractedly in Nick's direction. It sat on the surface of his face as if foreign to it, without any real warmth behind it—not that there was coldness either. Just the image of a smile projected on a screen. Nick wondered if he'd done it because someone had once told him it made him seem more approachable. They'd been wrong.

"Mr. Kurosawa. You're five minutes early."

"I could go out and come back in, if you wanted."

"That won't be necessary." Umber grabbed for his cane and rose from his seat with a little twitch of hesitation—no, it was pain, Nick realized. It was what the bland, projected smile had been meant to hide.

"You don't need to get up—" he started, but Umber cut him off with a gesture.

"I rather do, Mr. Kurosawa, or else I would have stayed seated. Sit down, please."

That shut Nick up; he sat. He watched Umber head into the back. For a few minutes, there was silence punctuated with some obscure, mechanical noises. Then he returned with two cups of coffee balanced on a silver tray—balanced one-handed, as the other was still driving his cane.

"Please," Umber said.

Nick took a cup. It was espresso, rich and creamy and dark.

"I like to have something to drink when I'm conducting business. If all goes well, of course, you'd be assisting me with tasks such as this from now on, so I will, in fact, not need to get up."

There was something in Umber's voice which made it hard to tell how serious he was being. Perhaps the thread of pain in his tone, Nick thought.

"For the next month, I would like to have you for twenty hours a week. That should be enough time to get used to each other, and for you to wrap up your other commitments. After that, should we both agree, I'd like to move you to full time. Forty hours, that is. It would be a salaried position, with occasional overtime."

He named the salary. Nick was glad he'd had the long disciplines of both the army and his doorman work to help him keep his face neutral. It was far better than he'd ever been paid, certainly far better than he'd expected.

"Is that level of compensation agreeable to you, Mr. Kurosawa?"

What was he expecting him to say—no, I won't do it for less than a million? Nick cleared his throat again. The coffee had somehow left it dryer than before. "You could afford a trained nurse for that."

"I could," Umber agreed. "But I choose to hire you instead. It isn't nursing I need."

Nick shifted in his chair. "You said if I took this job, you'd brief me on exactly what kind of work you would need."

"Indeed." He steepled his fingers. "In truth, what I need you for are the occasions which I cannot anticipate."

Nick took a breath. "Pardon me, Mr. Umber, but that's remarkably vague."

The smile flitted across his face again. This time, it seemed more genuine. "It is, isn't it? You'll have to pardon me some of that—accept it as an eccentricity. Are you comfortable driving, Mr. Kurosawa? Your Hawaii license is still valid, isn't it?"

It was a tangent he hadn't expected. "I can drive. I haven't for a few years, but if it's needed—"

"I prefer to travel by car if at all possible—I mean, to avoid air and train travel." Umber glanced away from Nick, then, almost as if he didn't want to meet his eyes. "There's one more thing. While I don't anticipate you will need to provide any medical services, the truth is that you may be the only person with me when there is a medical emergency."

"That's not a problem," Nick said. "I've had first aid training."

Umber narrowed his eyes slightly. "I know. I wasn't finished."

Nick inclined his head, a sudden nervous lump in his throat. There was something about Umber—some odd, teacherly attitude—that made him feel about two inches away from being in serious trouble at all times. "I'm sorry."

Umber nodded. "In a medical emergency you may need to act as my advocate. This means knowing, e.g., what medications I am on, what surgeries I have had."

Nick had never heard anyone say "e.g." out loud before. It was almost funny.

"I'll provide you a copy of the relevant paperwork. I expect you to read through it. And just so you are not confused by anything in the paperwork, you should know I am a transgender man."

Nick kept his face impassive, though his eyebrows wanted to shoot up by at least an inch. It wasn't as if he hadn't met a trans guy before, but most of them were...well, younger. And not in Westerley, which was not exactly a bastion of acceptance.

Umber looked at him sharply. "Is this an issue for you?"

"Not at all," Nick said.

"Good."

The last time a trans guy had come out to Nick, it'd been a hookup back in Hawaii, and he'd said...oh, something dumb, something like "Thank you for trusting me." The guy had taken it in the intended spirit, and they'd had a good time afterward. If he said something like "Thank you for trusting me" to Umber, he guessed he'd be out on the street in about two seconds flat.

Umber seemed gratified to drop the subject entirely. "Then all that remains is to fill out some paperwork and agree on your hours." He hesitated for a moment. "Actually, there is...one final thing."

Umber took out a manila folder from his desk. He slid out a file, about half an inch thick. Nick glanced at it, but he thought he'd already know what was inside. When Umber opened it, with a slow, deliberate flick of his wrist, he was not surprised by the photograph inside.

Christ. Was I ever that young?

Umber turned the file toward Nick and pushed it gently in his direction. A slight raise of the eyebrows served as invitation. Nick took the file and flicked through it. It was impressively thorough. Two-thirds of it was his military record, the rest his employment history, medical records, psychiatric evaluations...

"Some of these records are sealed," Nick said.

"Nothing is ever truly sealed," Umber said. "Not if you have the right access."

Nick almost laughed. Instead, he made a kind of huffing sound and turned the file back toward Umber. There was nothing in it that wasn't known to him, in any case. It was his life on the table.

"Nicholas Keoni Kurosawa," Umber said. "Born in Pearl City, Oahu to Kimo Kurosawa of same and Eleanor Richardson of Honolulu. Both deceased. Sister, Lily Kurosawa, also deceased. One aunt—"

"What's the point of this? Going to run down my own family history?"

Umber was silent a moment, then closed the file, tapping one well-manicured finger atop it. "Your CV did not include the circumstances of your discharge from the army."

"You didn't ask." He huffed again, not sure if he was offended or impressed. Possibly both. "Clearly you didn't need to."

"No," Umber admitted.

Nick wondered if it was meant to be a kind of threat: look at the shit I have on you. Or maybe Umber saw it as a kind of evening of the scales. There must have been a terrible vulnerability in sharing intimate information about your body with someone who was essentially a stranger. Well, he wasn't a stranger anymore. All of his life was summed up in a file roughly half an inch thick. It was depressing, really.

"I research everything very thoroughly," Umber said.

"I can see that." Nick's fingers were itching—he felt the restless need to punch something. Yet for some reason, the imagined target never resolved itself into Umber's face, which would have seemed the obvious choice. "I'm surprised you still want to hire me."

Umber's expression remained neutral. "I believe almost everyone deserves a chance to prove the best of themselves, Mr. Kurosawa. However, if you are uncomfortable with the lengths to which I go to research my employees, consider this your out."

Nick realized then what this had been. Not a threat, not an evening of the scales—a show of trust, in some bizarre way. Treat me fairly, and I'll treat you fairly, in my own way. "You've done your due diligence. I've taken you on faith."

Umber inclined his head. "Are you asking me for time to do your own, before you decide? I'll have to warn you, Mr. Kurosawa, not much of me is in the public record."

No, it wouldn't be, would it? "You did give a quote to the *Westerley Whisperer* a few months back."

"So I did." Umber's mouth quirked. "So it seems you have done at least some due diligence yourself. Don't tell me it's my politics that you take issue with."

Nick laughed a little. "No. Of course not."

Umber held Nick's eyes, waiting for the answer to his question—not bothering to ask it again.

Nick took a breath. "So, I believe you said something about working out my hours?"

*

Nick woke up at half past nine; in the winter, it felt like afternoon. The sun shone like polished steel in a gray sky. He washed and dressed while humming a tune he couldn't recall the words to.

He'd considered calling Mr. Umber in the morning and saying there wasn't any need to start on part time, that he didn't have any more night shifts at the Hellhole to worry about. He decided not to, though. This period of part time wasn't just to give him a chance to do his last set of night shifts. It was a probation as well, for both of them, and it seemed an inauspicious start to run roughshod over the terms Umber had set. He seemed a man who was serious about the rules he laid down.

Maybe that's why you like him so much, snickered some voice in the back of Nick's mind.

He frowned. *Fuck off—I don't like him, I respect him.*

"Arguing with yourself is the first sign of insanity, Kurosawa," he muttered.

He reached Umber's store—Umber's nameless store—at about half past two, which he judged was an allowable level of "gee boss, aren't I keen" and let himself in. The bell over the door tinkled. Again, there was nobody actually in the store; the place didn't exactly get the best footfall. Maybe it had ten, twenty, years ago when Margaret Mason owned it. Right now, it must be a money pit for Umber, unless he had some well-heeled clients coming in now and then, buying cow skulls and rusty old swords.

"Hello?" Nick called out. "Mr. Umber?"

There was a rustle from the back. Umber emerged, cane in hand—not the silver-tipped one he'd been carrying when they'd met near the Hellhole, but something plainer and more functional in polished wood. *The other one must be his dress cane.* Nick suppressed a smile at the thought.

"Mr. Kurosawa." He looked at his watch; he was one of the few men who actually wore a watch, rather than just checking his phone.

Nick shrugged awkwardly. "I know I'm a little early."

"No, this will suit just fine." Umber looked him up and down, his eyes oddly assessing.

Nick felt a little uncomfortable. "Am I not dressed for the job, or...?" He wore what he would have called business casual, but his sense of style had always been a little left of center. That had run in the family. His father had never worn anything other than Aloha shirts and khakis for work. He hadn't even been buried in a suit.

"No, you're more than fine, Mr. Kurosawa." Umber's mouth quirked a little. "If there is ever a need for more formal dress, I will be sure to let you know."

Nick's cheeks went warm. In most cases, he didn't show a blush, and right now, he was thankful for that. Somehow, though, he guessed Umber could sense it nonetheless. "All right. Uh, so, what do I do? I mean, I figured you'd want to start me with something simple."

"I thought for our first day you could assist me here in the store, and read through some documents." He paused a moment. "Tomorrow, you can start assisting me in my home."

"Whatever you think's best," Nick said. "You're the boss."

"Literally, yes," Umber said, so deadpan it took Nick a moment to recognize it as a joke. "Please, if you could make us both some coffee?"

"Sure thing—coffee machine is in the back, right?"

Umber nodded. "Have you used one before?"

Nick grinned a little. "Was a barista for about half a year in high school. I think I can manage."

"In that case, I'll leave it in your capable hands."

"How do you take it, Mr. Umber?"

"No milk, one cube of sugar, please."

Of course the sugar came in cute little lumps, in a sealed glass jar. There was something almost charmingly old-fashioned about the way Umber seemed to live his life, from the insistence on honorifics to his freshly ground coffee. It would have come off as an affectation in a different man, but somehow Umber landed closer to "charming old gentleman" than "insufferable hipster," mostly because there seemed to be nothing performative about it. He wasn't putting on a show. This was just how he lived his life.

Nick made two coffees and brought them over to Umber's desk. He noticed a little bronze disk of a coaster, and set Umber's coffee down on it. "Here you go."

"Thank you, Mr. Kurosawa. Here, could you go ahead and fill in these forms, please?" Umber handed him an honest-to-god clipboard, with a pen attached, and gestured to the easy chair where Nick had first seen him seated the day of his interview.

Nick took a seat, perched his coffee cup on a little half-moon shaped side table beside the chair, and got to filling out the forms Umber had handed him. He scribbled in his bank details, emergency contact (he put down Alex), tax information. So far, so much like any other job, Nick supposed. The first day was always settling in, filling out paperwork, and reading policy documents. Even in the army, that was pretty much par for the course.

He finished filling out the paperwork in about half an hour, around the same time it took him to drink his coffee.

Umber hadn't moved from his desk; he wrote in a ledger, the scratch of pen on paper the only sound in his store. After a while, he leaned back and sighed, looking up at Nick. "You've finished?"

He nodded. He couldn't help but sneak a look over Umber's shoulder at the ledger in front of him. It wasn't in any language, nor was it a simple sales record. It looked like a cipher. One line read something like "nfhr7 3289fgg 4fghg6 sdf74," all in a beautiful copperplate longhand, somehow more impressive for the fact that he'd been using a cheap ballpoint pen. "Here," Nick said, "I think that's all the information you need."

Umber glanced over it and nodded. "For the rest of today, you can assist in a stock-take of the store. If you do not mind."

Nick raised his eyebrows. "I'm not going to get precious."

Umber didn't smile but looked as if he could at any moment. "Then what you can assist with, Mr. Kurosawa, is completing a tally of all the fossils I have in the store." He handed Nick another clipboard, this one half-full with his neat copperplate. "They should all be labeled and boxed, but do let me know if you find any that have escaped."

"Sure thing," Nick said and glanced back over his shoulder. Umber was already buried back in his ledger.

Something like regret briefly twinged in Nick's chest. What swam to the surface, all incongruous, was *I would have liked to see him smile.*

Nick shook his head, dismissing the thought, and spent the next few hours combing through shelves' worth of knick-knacks, finding the fossils, and logging them in one of Umber's ledgers. Whether he'd have to type them up into a database later, Umber hadn't told him, but somehow, he didn't think so. Nick hadn't seen a computer or even a cell phone. Maybe Umber was one of the world's remaining technophobes. If Nick was right about his age, he was right on the cusp where it would have been possible to have grown up without any exposure to it. Nick himself, solidly millennial, would have rather chopped off a pinky than give up Internet access.

When Umber told Nick he could go home (after making him another coffee), it seemed almost as if no time had passed. He brought another coffee to Umber, setting it down on the bronze disk.

"Thank you for your help today, Mr. Kurosawa." Umber took a sip. "So far I have no complaints."

Damning with faint praise, Nick thought, but smiled. "Thank you for the opportunity, Mr. Umber."

He stood up to shake Nick's hand, his touch warm and deceptively strong. "I will see you tomorrow, Mr. Kurosawa. And...welcome."

It made him feel oddly warm, that welcome, with all its slightly stiff formality. As if he belonged here—as if he was valued. "Thanks," Nick said, a little gruffly, then added, "Mr. Umber," as a polite afterthought.

"Oh, and could you read through this tonight?" Umber handed him a slim envelope. "Bring them back tomorrow, please. It's my medical records, and some information about medical needs."

"Of course." Nick took the folder and held it, slightly awkwardly, under his arm. He hadn't brought a bag. "Have a good evening, Mr. Umber."

"And you, Mr. Kurosawa."

He went home with the same odd buoyancy as he'd had after he'd been formally hired. The kind of positive, things-are-looking-up feelings he felt only too rarely these days. It wasn't quite happiness—he was too leery to call it that—but it skirted the edge of it. *Well, I'll take what I can get.*

*

When Nick got home, he put his groceries away and sat down at the table, Umber's envelope in his hand. It wasn't glued shut, but tied with a neat little string. He opened it and slid out a stack of neatly printed letter-size paper. The medical records Umber had provided for him weren't medical records, exactly—at least, they didn't look as if they'd been prepared by any doctor's office. They looked as if Umber had written them up himself, in a dry, factual, third-person tone. There was a list of medications that he took and their dosages, most of them unfamiliar to Nick. Cyclobenzaprine, pregabalin, amitriptyline... The only ones he knew about were ibuprofen ("as needed") and testosterone ("testosterone undecanoate, one monthly injection").

In a small paragraph about past surgeries, Umber had listed a hysterectomy twenty years ago, a mastectomy one year after that, reconstructive surgery on his chest eight years ago, and two ligament reconstructions (left ankle, right knee) three and seven years ago, respectively, along with an exploratory bowel surgery. He must have almost as many scars as me, Nick though, half smiling.

His own medical record was clear enough on those: live-fire incident, nine years ago; knife wound, five years ago…

He suddenly thought of his pickup of a few years ago, the trans SoCal surfer boy on vacation. There weren't many commonalities—why would there be, when they only had being trans men in common—but his mind compared them nonetheless. Kirby. The boy's name suddenly came back to him. "Like the video game," he'd told Nick.

Nick had asked him a bunch of awkward questions about what he had in his pants. He supposed Umber's medical records told that story well enough and felt faintly ashamed for dwelling on the thought.

"Haven't had surgery except for my chest," Kirby had told him. "So I come with my factory-installed parts. If it's an issue for you fucking a man with a cunt…" He'd smiled and shrugged. "There's the door."

It hadn't been an issue for Nick. Kirby had first blown him, then pulled on his nipples until he whimpered, and finally pushed him down to enthusiastically ride his dick. A sudden sense-memory came back to Nick—Kirby grinning at him, grinding down on his cock, and then suddenly slapping him full in the face. He'd forgotten it had been him. Kirby had hidden a creatively sadistic streak under his beguilingly vulnerable, sun-washed twink exterior. No wonder Nick had liked him so much.

He read the other document Umber had included in the envelope, which ran through medical issues he might have on a daily basis. Pain and fatigue seemed to be the common elements. It was written in the same dry, factual tone as his medical information, but Nick thought he could detect cracks in the structure through which that pain shone, like dark light.

On some days, I will not require much assistance beyond possibly the moving of heavy objects. On other days, I will be unable to leave my apartment. On a few, I will be unable to leave my bedroom.

It was hard to reconcile what he'd written with the scrupulously put-together man Nick had begun to know, who didn't seem to leave his house without his suit pressed and every hair in place. But then, how many times had he seen him? Three, four? And never when the pain and stiffness and insomnia was at its the worst.

He put the records back in their envelope and resealed it, winding the thread back around the fixing. In a way, he now knew as much about Umber as Umber did about him, at least when it came to medical issues.

Depression with psychotic features—that had been down on Nick's paperwork. His discharge from the army had been medical; he'd had people looking out for him. They'd done the best they could. Saw the cracks, knew he was about to break. Without that diagnosis, it would have ended in court martial rather than being invalided out. Still, it wasn't something you wanted down in black-and-white for anyone diligent or clever enough to dig up.

Depression: he hated the word. He'd lived with it for most of his life, a quiet background visitor. His mother said he'd always been a moody kid. "You're all turned inward, Nicky," she'd said more than once. He just figured that his natural happiness level was set a little lower than most people's. It was like having to wear glasses, like having an organ that just didn't function at maximum efficiency. He could live with it, whether you called it depression or being moody or turning inward.

It wasn't like he was incapable of happiness. There was the first time he held his sister, or when a great song came on at a club, or the first time he'd kissed a boy. They blazed in his mind, almost more colorful for the grayness surrounding them.

Psychotic features, though—well, that had come later. After the news about his family. They'd pulled him out of a training exercise he was supervising, got a chaplain to give him the news. Nobody in their family had been religious except his Aunt Fiona, his mom's sister— she was the one who planned the funeral. Had them all buried before Nick could get home.

It had been a car accident. A dumb accident, with nobody, nothing to blame except a slippery road and a tight corner. The car rolled over a cliff. His mother and Lily were gone in an instant, and Aunt Fiona hadn't even buried them next to his father.

Nick had had a few weeks leave to put things in order. With the funeral arrangements all over and done with, that meant the house, their belongings. He told his aunt to go fuck herself. He sold the house. He donated everything that was left to charity, including Lily's toys. Then he went back on duty.

Six months later, he broke a rookie's nose and both cheekbones after he'd made some dumb-ass comment. Nick didn't remember what it was, only the black static hiss in his head when he'd been punching the man. And with that, he'd broken his career and what remained of his life. A lifetime of turning inward, and it took one outward turn to finally stamp a diagnosis on his records.

He should have asked for help. He knew that now. It hadn't been a sudden thing; it had crept up on him, the static buzz, the way the world made less and less sense, the way his gun sometimes seemed as if it could start talking to him with its prim, pursed *o* of a mouth. It could have gone a lot worse than the way it fell out, in the end. He knew that. The rookie he'd punched up made a full recovery, Nick got put on meds that helped bring that black static buzz down from a roar to a whisper—even if they also made him sluggish and numb—and the *o* of the gun's mouth stayed silent. He'd gone through six months of mandated therapy with a kind fifty-something woman named Dr. Flynn, who taught him the word for the thing he'd lived with his whole life: depression. He knew it made sense, had a medical precision to it, like calling a broken hand a metacarpal fracture. But he still kind of thought of it the way his mom did. Just being turned inward.

He'd been able to go off his meds over a year ago, with Dr. Flynn's blessing. There hadn't been much need to revisit that. The grief and horror had run its course, and he'd kept himself running along. Except things were starting to teeter on the edge a bit, weren't they? He winced. It was an uncomfortable realization.

"Some people cut themselves," Dr. Flynn had told him once, "and some people pull dangerous stunts, and some people"—this with a significant look at Nick—"start fights. But it comes down to the same things, which is that they're trying to numb out one kind of pain with another."

He hadn't been looking for fights, but he'd been letting them find him; he couldn't argue with that. The tedium, the emptiness, the lack of purpose... It had all been conspiring against him, not quite bringing back the black static of his worst days, but pushing him to...well. Not make the healthiest decisions.

He'd never told Dr. Flynn the details about what he liked to do, to have done to him, with the guys he met, but she'd gotten the broad strokes of it.

"Well, you could look at that in two ways," she'd said. "Either it's another way to replace one pain with another—and as coping mechanisms go, there are much worse ones you could pick—or it's a healthy way to enact a bit of...a bit of surrender."

"So it is healthy?" he'd asked.

"Anything can be unhealthy if it's done in an unhealthy way, Nick." She'd recommended some books to him—books he'd never read, for one reason or another. Maybe because he didn't want to give it any concrete shape, preferred to keep it something that happened by chance, in the dark. It scared him, to think it was something he could actually enjoy on a longer-term basis—scared him for reasons he couldn't quite put his finger on.

He shook his head, clearing away the fog of memories. He'd meant to get to the gym; he needed it, needed some kind of endorphin kick. If he couldn't get a good fuck, or a good flogging, then a good half hour on a rowing machine and another on the treadmill would have to do. He slid Umber's file across the table, as if there were an invisible man there waiting to take it, then got dressed in his gym clothes and headed out the door.

*

After the gym, he'd gone home and slept like the dead, waking up fresh for his second day at work. That day was more of the same—fossil hunting in the store—except that after Umber's second coffee, he closed up the store and told Nick to accompany him home. "I'm shutting a little early today," he said, "so that you can get a sense of the routine without going over your hours."

"It's fine if you want to stay until your usual closing time," Nick said. "I don't have anywhere to be." He felt a little awkward the moment after saying it, as if it was something you weren't supposed to admit to your boss.

"No," Umber said, pushing his chair away from his desk. "I'm done for the day, I think, and it would be counterproductive, leaving you to close up the store when I need you with me at home today."

Nick noticed a slight stiffness in Umber's movements, a shadow under his eyes that wasn't usually there. "Shall I call a taxi, Mr. Umber?"

"I've already ordered one, Mr. Kurosawa, but thank you."

He hadn't heard Umber on the phone with anyone. Nick wondered if he'd ordered the taxi before he'd even arrived, knowing that he'd have to shut up early. Knowing that he'd have to conserve his energy.

A black car was waiting for them, idling at the curb opposite the store. They got in, both in the back seat. The driver looked back; he was perfectly ordinary, neither cop nor gangster, as far as Nick could tell. "Where to?"

"Clarebrook Towers, please."

Nick's eyebrows rose. Clarebrook Towers was Westerley's most luxe apartment complex, built five years ago to attract high-powered businessmen and B-class celebrities. Somehow, regardless of how well Umber paid him, Nick expected him to live somewhere more...well, humble. He had class, Nick couldn't argue with that, but it wasn't flashy. It seemed to be out of its element in the glass-and-metal jut of Clarebrook.

"Clarebrook Towers," Umber said, turning toward him, "has the best options for security in Westerley, unless one were to buy a house and outfit it oneself."

Fuck, am I that easy to read? "Not that I can judge," he said.

Umber's mouth quirked. "You will be able to, in a moment."

The taxi dropped them at the front entrance. A reception desk sat in the middle of the lobby with a guard-cum-receptionist on duty. He waved them through with a tight little smile in Umber's direction. Automatically, Nick checked the place for alternative exits. There weren't any in plain sight, but that didn't mean they didn't exist. He doubted the man at the desk came and left through the front door when his shifts started and ended.

If the facade of Clarebrook Towers was a grand, if slightly tacky, beacon, the interior was all understated elegance. Nick had expected it to look like a plush hotel, but it was tasteful to the edge of blandness. A raft of elevators took up most of the vestibule with three on each side and one at the far end, slightly smaller than the rest. He wasn't entirely surprised when Umber walked to the last elevator and swiped the reader beside it with a silvery card.

"Penthouse elevator," he explained.

Of course, Nick thought, but he kept his mouth shut.

The elevator shuddered to a halt and opened into a short, wide corridor, with the same understated decor as the lobby. The locks on the door were impressive. A keypad as well as two Yale locks, each requiring a separate key.

"You weren't kidding about the security," Nick said.

"Oh, the locks are the least of it," Umber said, taking out his keys. "There is round-the-clock surveillance on the building."

"Lifestyles of the rich and paranoid," Nick joked without thinking.

Umber half laughed. "Indeed."

"Sorry, I—"

"No, you're quite right, Mr. Kurosawa." Umber unlocked the second lock, keyed in a code, and pushed open the door.

Nick wasn't sure what he'd expected from Mr. Umber's penthouse. It'd be one thing or the other, he had supposed: harsh and spartan minimalism, or peacock-feather fans and jaguar-skin rugs everywhere, maybe with a butler named Jeeves wearing nothing except a jockstrap and nipple pasties. *Probably not the latter, though.* The thing that struck Nick about it most was how normal it seemed. The way anyone might outfit their apartment, just a little...nicer.

He followed Umber through the hallway and into what he assumed was the living room. An ordinary living room. Leather sofa, a flat-screen television—why had he assumed Umber wasn't the type to own a television?—and a deep-piled Turkish rug. A vaguely pre-Raphaelite painting hung on the wall, of a woman with red hair looking out over a stormy sea.

"Could you assist me with my coat, please?"

Nick took Umber's coat off his shoulders. Umber was moving a little stiffly, not quite in pain, but as if he were being careful to avoid it. "Where should I hang it?"

"Second door to the right is my bedroom. Hang it in the wardrobe, if you please." Umber sat down on the sofa with a heavy sigh.

Nick nodded and made his way to the bedroom. A small, dark thrill went through him—the thrill of sneaking somewhere he shouldn't go. It didn't make much sense; Umber had just told him to go inside. Still, there was something shadowy-intimate about it, about going into another person's bedroom without them.

If he'd been looking for minimalism, Umber's bedroom almost hit the mark. It wasn't what you might call spartan, not with the luxurious bedding, but apart from the sizeable wardrobe and a small nightstand, there was nothing to give a hint to its inhabitant's character. It looked oddly empty, even with the massive bed.

When he returned, Umber's eyes were closed.

Nick shifted from foot to foot. After a few moments, he cleared his throat. "Is there anything I can do for you, Mr. Umber?"

"Absolutely." His voice was distant, with pain or exhaustion or both.

The silence went on a beat too long.

"Please," Umber said, speaking slowly, "could you fetch the black case from the master bathroom? And make me a cup of tea."

"Black case," Nick echoed. "Got it."

The light came on automatically, a gentle bloom of orange that eventually became a buttery yellow-white. Made to save eyesight at night, Nick guessed; it was a nice touch. It reminded Nick of a hotel bathroom, impersonally clean, the bright white towels hung with geometrical precision. The black case that Umber mentioned was on one side of the sink, dominating it, almost as large as a toolbox. He picked it up, surprised at how light it actually was, and took it into the living room.

Umber's eyes were still closed. He didn't react when Nick set the black case down on the coffee table. Nick went back into the kitchen and made the tea. He poured a cup, then realized he hadn't asked Umber how he took it.

He poked his head back into the living room. "Mr. Umber? Do you have it with milk, or lemon, sugar…?"

"It depends what sort of tea it is," he said, not turning to face Nick.

"Earl Grey." There had been a bewildering array of teas in Umber's cupboards. Nick had picked the most familiar.

"Lemon and a little sugar, then, please."

He found the sugar, measured out half a teaspoon, and squeezed a few drops of lemon juice into the teacup. Then he brought teacup and saucer into the living room and set it down gently next to the black case. "Here you go," he said.

Umber opened his eyes slowly. "Thank you," he said and sat up straighter and opened the black case to reveal a pharmacy's worth of pills, neatly arranged like gems in a lady's jewelry box: ruby cabochons and white diamonds, sapphires banded with ebony, and amber bottles filled with tiny pearls. He measured out two of those pearls, and one white diamond, and tipped all three into his mouth, washing them down with a mouthful of tea. Then he closed the case. "Can you please return this to the bathroom?"

"Of course." Nick took the case and put it back where he found it.

When he returned to the living room, Umber looked marginally less like he was about to go into hibernation, sitting upright and sipping at his cup of tea.

"Is there anything else I can do for you?" Nick felt vaguely uncomfortable just being in his presence without doing something.

He nodded. "There is a menu for a Chinese takeout in one of the kitchen drawers. Can you call and order me a number twenty-seven with noodles? If you'd like, you can order something for yourself before you go home."

Nick shook his head. "That's all right. Thank you, Mr. Umber."

"In that case, if you would take the garment bag hanging in the walk-in closet to Avery's laundry service on Jackson Avenue and bring it to the store tomorrow afternoon."

"Is that all?"

"That's all, Mr. Kurosawa."

It didn't seem worth the salary Umber was paying him. It was simple things, things that he could have easily done for a friend, even the fossil sorting. From what Umber had told him, though, and from what he'd read in the man's medical files, it could get complicated easily enough.

Nick ordered the food and took the garment bag. Umber was still sitting on the sofa, his cup of tea empty on the coffee table.

"Shall I put that in the kitchen?"

"Please."

As he was about to leave, Nick looked back toward Umber—toward the back of his head. He suddenly regretted saying no to the offer of takeout. Bit strange, though, eating dinner with your boss…though from his reading, it wasn't uncommon for PAs to dine with their employers, sometimes to help them with their food. No, the reason he'd said no wasn't because it would have been strange. It was because he'd wanted to say yes—and hadn't trusted the impulse. "I'll see you tomorrow, Mr. Umber."

"Indeed, you will, Mr. Kurosawa. Have a good evening."

He smiled briefly, as if he hadn't intended to. "And you."

*

It almost amazed Nick how quickly he fell into Umber's routine—it was as if the job had been waiting for him, a missing piece of a puzzle he'd snapped into with satisfyingly effortless ease. After a week, Umber said that if it was amenable to Nick (he used that word: amenable), he would cut short their probation period and take Nick on full-time. Nick agreed instantly; the job suited him to a tee.

Part of him had thought being a personal assistant would be hard, and sometimes it was...challenging. The hours of waiting, of dead time, until he might or might not be needed—those were the worst for him. Sometimes, it was almost like a retail job with extra bits bolted on, although the number of actual customers Umber's store had could be counted on two hands in as many weeks. Mostly, he was just there, when Umber needed him.

There was something...gratifying about it though. As long as there was enough variation in what Umber asked—and there was—Nick didn't mind being his hands in the world. He thought it could go on like this, with him somewhere between a stock boy, gofer, and occasional nurse, until the day Umber changed the script.

"We'll be closing early today," he said when Nick arrived for his shift. "We are going out."

"Where are we heading?"

"To see..." Umber paused for a moment, searching for words. "To see a client of mine. Could you get my coat, Mr. Kurosawa? The tweed Chesterfield, if you please."

Nick had no idea what a Chesterfield was, but he knew what tweed was, and only one tweed coat hung on the rack. He took it and helped Umber into the coat. "Do you want me to call a taxi?"

"No, we'll be walking." Umber unlocked a drawer and took out a thick manila envelope, tucked it in his inner coat pocket before locking the drawer again, and retrieved his cane from an umbrella stand beside the door. "Follow me."

They left the store behind. Umber walked with a deliberate pace, not slow, exactly, but judged. He led the way with the confidence of a man who knew the streets from long familiarity. Nick had only been in Westerley for a year and floundered behind him like a tourist—though it didn't show, or at least he hoped it didn't. He'd fallen into a rhythm now, matching Umber's strides.

Nick's interest was piqued. Unless he sold some extremely high-ticket items now and then, it didn't seem enough people came into Umber's store for it to be his sole source of income. Not with the salary he was paying Nick, that was for sure. Maybe this would give him some sort of clue.

They wound through back streets Nick had never seen before. Dark, almost Victorian buildings with rusted fire escapes reared up before them, twisting the city streets into narrow alleys—it was as if they'd suddenly walked into a different city. Nick had always thought of Westerley as a bland place, but this part of the city was anything but bland. It had an edge to it, jagged and ungentrified. Not a few of the buildings were boarded up, or daubed with faded graffiti.

Eventually, they reached their destination: a run-down apartment building, the front door a heavy metal slab. Umber tilted his head in the door's direction. "This is the place," he said.

"Stay behind me." Old habits—Nick pushed the door open, checking out the surroundings. In the gloom of the lobby, a shaggy-haired man was slumped against the wall. A woman peered at him from the landing above and retreated quick as a ghost when he looked up. It seemed like a shithole, but not immediately dangerous. If the shaggy-haired guy went after the two of them—if he was awake enough to try it—Nick was sure he could take him. Unless the guy had a gun. Then all bets were off.

The guy didn't get up. Umber jerked his head upward. "Fifth floor," he said.

"No elevator?"

Umber smiled thinly. "What do you think?"

It was more stairs than Umber would usually climb. Nick reached to support him on the way up. Umber paused, for half a moment, looking back at Nick over his shoulder. His eyes met Nick's—a momentary wariness deepened into warmth. "Thank you, Mr. Kurosawa," he said.

Nick's stomach flipped, suddenly too aware of their proximity, of the sea-glass beauty of Umber's dark eyes. Then he turned away. Nick realized he'd been holding his breath and let it out in a quiet sigh.

The building looked as if it had been beautiful, once. There were slight art deco touches here and there, grimed with years of dirt, and light fixtures that might have bathed the entire place in golden lamplight if they hadn't been broken.

"Looks like this might have been a nice place."

"It was," Umber said. "But the current owner would rather not invest the money needed to fix it. Here we are."

The door was marked 408. Umber knocked on it three times. It opened a crack, showing a gleam of the lock chain and a thin, haggard woman's face.

"Maria Jacubs?"

She nodded warily.

"We've corresponded. I am Mr. Umber."

Her eyes lit with recognition, and an unsteady smile made her face look suddenly younger. Beneath the haggardness, she might have been as young as twenty. "Mr. Umber," she said; she had a slight Eastern European accent. "Please come in."

The door closed for a moment, with the rattle of the chain being unlatched. She opened it again. She was very skinny, wearing a floral-print dress and sensible black shoes.

"I'm sorry I don't have anything to offer you," she said, a touch of wariness in her voice. "I—I am of course very grateful."

"There's no need to offer me anything," Umber said. "As I said over the phone, this is purely done as a favor."

She laughed mirthlessly. "In my experience, Mr. Umber, favors are very rarely without strings."

He nodded. "Right you are."

"So here I am, looking for the strings."

He fished the envelope from his coat and handed it to her. She tore it open with something that could have been greed, or desperation, and tipped the contents into her palm. Nick saw something that looked like a passport, several plasticky cards, like credit cards, and some very official-looking paperwork, complete with stamps and seals. Her eyes went wide at it.

"The strings, Miss Jacubs, are very simple. Take advantage of your new opportunity with haste, and forget my name."

"Why are you doing this?" Her voice was hoarse with emotion. "There is nothing I can do to repay you."

"Then perhaps," Umber said, "you will one day do a kindness on my behalf, to someone else in need."

She made a gesture that was almost a curtsy and said something in a language Nick didn't understand.

"You're welcome," Umber said. "Mr. Kurosawa, let us leave Miss Jacubs in peace."

*

They left, winding back down the apartment building stairs. The shaggy-haired man was still there, his eyes glazed. Nick wondered vaguely if they should call an ambulance.

They managed to make it three blocks in silence before Umber turned to him with a quizzically raised eyebrow. "Go ahead and ask, Mr. Kurosawa. I know you're dying to."

Nick coughed. "Dying to ask what?"

"Come now," Umber said. "Don't play dumb. It does not suit you in the slightest."

Backhanded compliment if I ever heard one. "All right, I'm asking. What, exactly, is it that you do?"

Umber smiled a little—that thin, ironic tilt of his mouth that passed for his smile, in any case. "What any good businessman does. I provide things that my clients want, or need."

"Most clients tend to pay businessmen. Unless I'm really mistaken in what was going on there, that woman didn't pay you."

"No." The smile slowly faded from his face. "I am gladly well off enough to subsidize some...pro bono work."

"Pro bono work," Nick echoed.

"A few essential papers, in this case."

Some instinct prickled at the nape of his neck, raising the hairs there in the presentiment of danger—some mild danger, maybe, but it was there, anyway. It made sense that Umber had some other means of income besides the store. Nick had vaguely assumed it was a trust fund of some kind. This made it seem like it was something less than legal.

Come off it, a ticked-off voice responded. Did he seem like a criminal? Did he look like he was exploiting that woman? No, she'd been too grateful for that. She hadn't even paid him. Still, it added up to some more than vague shadiness.

Nick was still chewing on it when he noticed Umber had fallen behind him a bit. He slowed his step and waited for him to catch up. "Are you all right, Mr. Umber?"

He took a deep breath and looked up at Nick as if gaging whether or not to tell the truth. "No," he said finally. "I'm beginning to have a bad flare-up. Could you please get me home as quick as—as—"

"Not a problem," Nick said, cutting Umber off before he had to struggle for more words. He took his arm—it was an instinctive gesture—and steered him gently across the street, where he'd spotted a quiet-looking cafe. He led him to a table and went to buy him a cup of tea while on his phone to Umber's preferred taxi company. "Yeah, Common Grounds on Reddish Street. Ten minutes? Great, all right."

He hung up and brought the tea to Umber, who sipped at it gratefully. His eyes still looked unfocused, half glazed over. Nick had seen eyes like that in the mirror in the first few weeks on his meds, when it felt he'd been run over by a dump truck, when it was too much effort to even string words together coherently. It was a kind of tiredness that went bone-deep, and it had come over Umber with frightening rapidity.

"Mr. Umber?" He spoke softly, almost reticent, as if Umber was a wild thing he didn't want to spook. "I've called a cab. It'll be here in ten minutes."

He found Nick's eyes. "Thank you." It seemed to cost him some effort to say it.

"Drink your tea," Nick said. For a moment, he had an absurd impulse to reach out and stroke Umber's hand, to give him an anchor of touch. He restrained himself and rallied by blustering about getting a coffee for himself. He hadn't thought to get anything earlier, when he'd gotten Umber's tea.

Truthfully, he didn't even really want anything, but it covered over the moment of extreme awkwardness. He returned with an espresso, but a moment after he'd sat down, he got the notification the taxi was outside. He got up again. "Taxi's here."

Umber looked up at him. His tea was half unfinished. "All right," he said in the same slow, strange, halting way he'd said thank you.

Nick went to his side and offered his arm. Umber took it and dragged himself upright. They got into the taxi, and Nick directed them back to Clarebrook Towers. Once they were on the way, something seemed to sharpen up again in Umber's eyes; he didn't look as if he were lost anymore. He just looked very, very tired. He sighed heavily and sagged back against the seat of the cab. Nick didn't want to speak—didn't want to interrupt whatever recovery was going on—so they rode to the apartment in silence.

He gave his arm again to get him out of the car and into the elevator. When they reached the apartment a kind of shudder went through Umber.

"Could you...please assist me to my office?" he asked. Nick nodded. He'd not been into Umber's home office yet, but he knew which door it was. He helped steady Umber on his way there and opened the door for him.

He wasn't sure what he'd expected, but it wasn't this. An old-fashioned typewriter on a big wooden desk, maybe. The desk was big enough, and wooden, but modern in design rather than the old bureau he had at the store, and instead of a typewriter, he had a sleek, multimonitor computer setup. Two keyboards as well, both fancy mechanical ones, one of them a massive slab that could have been at home in a nuclear submarine. *So much for being a technophobe.*

Umber sat himself down in his desk chair, an ergonomic beast of black leather, and let out a long sigh.

"Are you all right?"

"Sometimes this happens," he said. "I will be fine for hours, an entire day...weeks. Then it comes crashing in all at once, and all I can do is go home. Collapse."

Nick nodded. It made sense to him, from what he'd read. "Are you hungry? Thirsty? I could make you dinner."

Umber shook his head slightly. "No, what I need now is to be alone. Please, it is no offense to you; I will be able to order dinner shortly, after some rest." Umber looked up from his desk and smiled at Nick. That warmth was back in his gray-green eyes. "You've been invaluable today, Mr. Kurosawa. I'm not sure how I could have done it without you."

Nick inclined his head. "That's why you hired me, Mr. Umber."

He went home without thinking much more of it. It was only when he was halfway through his dinner that he realized where the warm, comfortable glow that had nestled under his breastbone had come from: that almost-affectionate look in Umber's eyes, the hint of a smile. *I'm not sure how I could have done it without you.*

He had to cover his face with his hands in sheer embarrassment. *Shit, shit. Don't fucking tell me I'm falling in love with my boss.*

Part Two

NEGOTIATIONS

"In love" might have been a strong phrase. Nick wasn't sure if he'd ever really been in love with anyone, but it was becoming all too clear he was developing a crush on Jacob Umber. For a few days, he tried to convince himself otherwise, that it was nothing more than admiration for a man who was tough as old boot-leather underneath his urbane exterior. That he felt for Umber what he might feel for a mentor or a role model, combined with the pleasure of a job well done.

It would have been easier if he'd managed to convince himself of that, but he wasn't quite that skilled at self-deception. The truth was that something about Jacob Umber didn't just appeal to him, it haunted him. When he was with Umber, he felt...content, right, happy almost. When he left for the day to go back to his empty apartment, it was like the weather changing. It left the world colder than it should be, with the memory of sunshine haunting him like the gentle touch of warm hands on bare shoulders.

Now he was lying in bed trying to sleep, and the thought wouldn't leave him: he wanted Umber.

Part of it was that he was being useful; he couldn't deny that. He did help Mr. Umber, in an immediate and visible sense, and it gave him some irreducible satisfaction to do so. It was the same kind of satisfaction he got in the Army, at the end of a day, when everything had gone to plan, and people had thumped his shoulders and said "Good work today, Kurosawa," or "We sure showed them today, huh, Nick?" That part didn't necessarily mean anything about his feelings for Umber…except that it had all gotten tangled together in his head, the usefulness and the happiness and the way that looking into Umber's sea-glass eyes made his stomach flip, as if he were a teenager with his first crush.

It was stupid, of course. Even if Umber were interested in him, could be interested in him—and that was a big "if"—they were employer and employee. Boss and PA.

God, but wouldn't it be something if he told me to just…get on my knees, one day at the store. "Open your mouth, Mr. Kurosawa, if you please. Yes, that's very good." Nick bit the back of his hand to stop himself from making a sad little moaning sound. *Fuck. I'm in deep, here.*

Well, there wasn't anything for it except to ignore it until it went away. He'd crushed on unsuitable men before—men who were straight, or in his chain of command, or just plain bad news. In all cases, the feeling had faded after a few weeks, and he'd moved on to someone else, someone better, a Mr. Right Now to distract him.

Something clicked in his head. That was what he needed. A distraction. He remembered the card Gordon had given him a few weeks back before he'd started working for Umber. He got out of bed and checked it was still tucked into his wallet. What had Gordon said—last

Friday of the month? That was in four days. It'd make a good distraction, something to clear his head, some rough-handed man to erase the ghost-image of Umber's eyes, the echoes of his voice.

Nick's phone rang—he jumped out of bed as if he'd been caught at something, heart hammering in his throat. It wasn't Umber, though; it was Alex.

"Hey." Nick's voice was a little shaky when he answered, but he covered it by faking a momentary cough and then saying "hey" again. "How are you?"

"Hey, Nick," Alex said. "Haven't heard from you in a couple of weeks."

With a burst of realization that bordered on shame, Nick suddenly knew he hadn't talked to Alex for weeks. He'd been neck-deep in his new job—his new obsession. He groaned under his breath, rubbing his face. "Shit, you're right. I'm sorry, Alex. I should have called you."

"You're all right, though?"

"Yeah—yeah, I'm all right."

"That's good." The warmth in Alex's voice made another spike of guilt go through him.

"The new job is going well," Nick said.

"Oh—did you get the job with Jacob Umber?"

He nodded, then remembered that was fairly useless over the phone. "Yeah, I did. I owe you a big favor."

"No, you don't," Alex said fondly. "But I wouldn't say no to drinks. How about meeting at the Hellhole tomorrow?"

Nick groaned under his breath. "The Hellhole, again, really?"

"I know you've been enjoying your time away," Alex said with the slightest touch of sarcasm in his voice, "but I happen to be fond of the place. Not to mention, I think it's important that we support our community."

"All right, all right. You talk like a fucking politician, you know that, Alex?"

"Maybe I'd make a pretty good one."

"Yeah, well, you'd have to give up on your little projects. Like me."

"Nonsense," Alex said. "I'd just be expanding my projects."

Nick laughed softly. "Sure."

"The Hellhole," Alex said again. "Eight o'clock tonight, before the crowds show up. What do you say?"

"Make it nine," Nick said. "I don't get off work until eight." His usual shift was two to eight, Monday to Saturday, a pattern that suited him and Umber both.

"Nine it is. I'll see you then."

"See you then, Alex."

There was a click and then dead air. Nick ran his hand through his hair. Between his racing thoughts and Alex's unexpected phone call, he wasn't sure how he'd get back to sleep tonight. He checked his phone—it was almost midnight. Late, for Alex to call, though early for Nick to be in bed. He wondered if Alex's intent had been for a booty call—if something he'd heard in Nick's voice had put him off. For a moment, he considered calling Alex back, making the offer. But it seemed wrong somehow. Not with thoughts of Umber still buzzing through his head, that pernicious fantasy of going down on his knees for him.

An errant thought spiked through his mind. *Does he use a strap-on cock? He could be any size he wanted to be.* Nick tried to slam a lid on that thought, but once it had come up, it was hard to dismiss. He thought of Umber undoing the buttons of his fly, drawing out a smooth and massive cock. "No, Mr. Kurosawa, I don't think that will do. I think you will need something bigger."

With a moan of frustration, Nick stripped off what was left of his clothes and jumped in the shower. He wanted the roar of the water to drown out his thoughts, to erase Umber's image. The last thing he needed was to start popping boners every time he was around his boss. He jerked himself off with brutal efficiency, using the long-practiced strokes he'd learned trying to get off quick and quiet in the barracks. Whenever another treacherous image of Umber rose up, he forced it away, thinking of anything else. Fucking Alex, getting sucked off in a rocky cave on a small beach by a surfer, his first drill instructor…

Being taken over Umber's lap, spanked with his thick leather belt.

Fuck. His body betrayed him, coming with a spasm the moment he let the thought creep back in. He breathed heavily, gasping under the torrent of water. He rinsed off quickly, toweled dry with rough efficiency, and slid into bed, his heart still pounding, his cock still half-hard. Fuck, he thought again, throwing an arm over his eyes.

Give it a couple of weeks, Kurosawa. You'll be over him before you know it.

*

Somehow, Nick managed to get through the day without embarrassing himself. Whatever fucked-up crush on Jacob Umber his brain had generated, it also seemed to be smart enough not to drop him completely into bullshit. He was able to get through his day acting, even feeling mostly normal, and when Umber wished him a good night, he almost breathed out a sigh of relief. It was a good sign; it meant that whatever this was, it was survivable. Ignorable.

He took a taxi to the Hellhole—somehow hailing a cab was always easy when he'd come out of Clarebrook Towers. He felt a little bit like a traitor, getting out, feeling the door supervisor's eyes on him. *That was me a few weeks ago*. He didn't know this guy; it must have been his replacement.

Alex was waiting for him at the bar, a gin and tonic already in hand. The blacklight bulb over the bar made it glow like a sci-fi concoction in the dimness of the club. Alex raised his glass. "The man of the hour," he said and took a sip. "What can I get for you?"

Nick smiled. "Are you buying this round?"

"Sure." Alex set his G & T down and waved Dominic, the bartender, over. Nick ordered a dark and stormy, his favorite drink. They toasted, clinking their glasses together, and Alex ordered a tonic with lemon to follow up ("Pacing myself tonight," he said), and they retreated to one of the booths. It was still early in the evening, and there were only a few regulars straggling around the place, trading gossip or watching the televisions mounted over the bar, waiting for possible new meat to wander in.

"Hey, sorry I didn't get in touch earlier," Alex said once they'd sat down. "I've been a bit busy these last few weeks."

"That's all right," Nick said. "I've been pretty busy myself, to tell you the truth."

Alex tilted his head, looking at Nick with uncomfortable intensity. After a while, he laughed. "I'll be damned, you actually mean that."

Nick drew back a little, frowning "What's that supposed to mean?"

"Hey, come on. I didn't mean it in a bad way. Just that...the last few times you've said 'that's all right,' and that you've 'been busy,' I could tell you were lying to me."

"I see." Nick made a sour face. "You didn't point it out at the time, of course."

"I didn't think it was worth starting a fight about," Alex said gently, putting his hand on top of Nick's. "I'm happy you're doing well, Nick, that's all."

Nick pulled his hand away but managed a smile. "Well, I am doing well."

"You almost sound surprised."

"I am, a little."

"Is it the job? Suits you better than doorman work, I bet."

Nick chewed on it for a moment. "It does suit me better. But it wasn't what I expected." He laughed. "Honestly, I'm not sure what I expected in the first place, but whatever it was, this isn't it."

Alex leaned back, smiling. "So tell me about it."

Nick mirrored him, leaning back against the seat of the booth and looking off into the middle distance a moment. Trying to figure out a way to summarize the last few weeks of working for Jacob Umber. "I'm not sure where to start."

"The usual place is at the beginning," Alex deadpanned.

"Well, you know the beginning! You're the one who pointed me in Umber's direction." He looked sideways at Alex. "Where did you meet him, anyway?"

Alex smiled a little. "Here, in the Hellhole. I know, you wouldn't think it to look at him, would you? So straitlaced."

Nick's eyes narrowed. "He one of your pickups? Doesn't seem your type, really."

"Why, you jealous?" Alex teased.

Nick grimaced and crossed his legs.

"You are!"

"I'm not jealous. I'm curious."

"No, he wasn't one of my 'pickups'—not like you." Alex gave him a sidelong smile. "I have to admit, I'm a little surprised. It's not me you're jealous of, that much I know, but if Mr. Umber isn't my type, he's sure as hell not yours either."

"I'm just—" Nick huffed out an irritated breath. "So he wasn't a pickup. That mean you just, what, got to talking? At three AM, with the music pounding?"

"It's not always three AM with the music pounding, you know," Alex said reproachfully. "Sometimes it's nice to just...be among friends. Have a talk with men who you know will understand a little about your life."

Nick snorted. "And you think Jacob Umber understands your life?"

"He certainly seems to be able to listen, which is more than I can say for a lot of men. Including you, sometimes."

Nick held up his hands. "Sorry. Go on."

"So, yes, we just got to talking. I talked about my work, and how I wish Westerley had a more active gay community—not a hook-up culture, an actual community, you know. I like it here, but there are people who'd rather not do their socializing in a bar."

"Who could blame them."

Alex ignored him. "And he told me about running his antique business, and how it doesn't leave him much energy, with his illness."

His antique business. For a moment, Nick debated telling Alex about the store. About how little it seemed to figure in Umber's actual daily life, about how it had been bought wholesale from a dead woman. But some instinct stopped him.

"So, I take it the job is working out better than anticipated?"

"No complaints on my part, so far," Nick said. "It's well paid." Understatement, he thought. "And it's...interesting."

"That's the most important thing, isn't it? To feel you've got a reason for going to work in the morning. Or evening."

"Yeah." Nick traced the rim of his glass with the edge of a knuckle. "I missed that. I didn't realize how much. I guess I owe you thanks."

Alex smiled. "No need for it. Seeing you happy is thanks enough."

They had a few more drinks together, the night getting warmer and blurrier at the edges with each one, and somewhere in between those drinks, Nick realized Alex had been flirting with him. It was subtle, little touches here and there, sidelong smiles, not the usual blunt way that men in the Hellhole cruised one another. Alex had always been a little subtler. Usually, Nick would be responding, especially with a few drinks in him. Alex was good-looking, a good friend, a conscientious lover. But something in Nick seemed to not be moving right, some stuck gear in his works that made the thought of going home with Alex seem cold and unappealing.

Maybe it was just that he wasn't in the mood for Alex's gentleness, for the good-natured tussle of who was going to top, for the easy friendliness of it. Maybe it was that he wanted something rougher, darker-edged.

Or maybe it was that every time he thought of someone's hand on him, it turned into Umber's.

Nick slowed down on drinking, bought Alex a cola or two, and started the process of extricating himself. Alex was disappointed, but only a little—there had never been any real heat between them, only a friendship with a sometimes-sexual edge. The edge had been blunted for Nick, though, perhaps forever. Alex would make some man very happy, Nick was sure of that, his Mr. Right or Mr. Right Now. But he and Alex were better off staying out of each other's bed.

What Nick needed would have to wait until Friday.

*

Three days came and went, and the way Nick felt about Umber stubbornly refused to change.

On Wednesday, they had their first drive across state lines. Umber had a meeting with a client in a city only slightly bigger but much more prestigious than Westerley which would have been about half an hour's flight from the nearest airport. It was a four-hour drive in a rented car.

For some reason, Nick had thought he'd sit up front and Umber would sit in the back, a chauffeur and his very proper client, but Umber sat next to him in the front seat, and the whole drive there, Nick's hand had tingled every time he changed gears and reached into what he saw as the bubble of Umber's personal space.

Not that he didn't enter that space almost every day, taking Umber's coat off, helping him with his shoes, supporting him a few times when climbing stairs. But he could be professional, then, shut off whatever was going on in his head that made him want to touch Umber. It wasn't so easy when there wasn't a specific reason to be in that halo of space. When all he wanted was for Umber to reach over and put his hand on top of Nick's.

When Friday came around and he asked if he could take an early day, it was almost a relief when Umber distractedly told him "That's fine" and dismissed him, even though something inside Nick twinged like a hurt nerve at being so easily sent away. Fucking childish, he told himself, and went home to prepare for the kink night Gordon had told him about.

He washed, shaved, doused himself in cologne, and combed his hair to ruler-straightness. When he looked at himself in the mirror, he saw someone good-looking enough, but sharpened by desperation. He almost laughed. They'd probably smell it on him when he walked in.

The address Gordon had given him on that oil-slick-rainbow card turned out to be a brownstone in a shabby-upscale neighborhood. Gordon hadn't mentioned anything about a dress code, so Nick had played it safe: neat black chinos, tight black T-shirt, leather jacket, well-polished boots. Just on the right side of deniable, in other words.

The door was unmarked. It looked like an ordinary house. Standing on the curb, Nick was tempted to cut his losses. The hollow, needy ache in his chest and the hopeful stir of his cock in his tight trousers said different, though. He walked up the steps and rang the doorbell.

About three minutes later, just when he was debating with himself whether to ring the bell again or walk away, the door opened. The man who answered was just a little too neatly dressed for a quiet night in, and his tie was leather. If not for those little hints, Nick would have thought he was in the wrong place. "Yes?"

Nick proffered the card. "Gordon gave me one of these? He said this might be my kind of night."

The man's look turned from cautious to nakedly appreciative, raking shamelessly over Nick's body. "Of course," he said, "come on in. A friend of Gordon's is a friend of ours."

With the door closed, Nick could hear a low thrum of music coming from deeper inside the house. It was someone's house, that much was plain, but the lights had been turned down low, and there was a smell in the air Nick recognized at once, a thick, back-of-the-throat smell, a mix of sex and leather, of rubber and sweat.

"I'm Jake," the man said, holding out his hand.

Nick shook it. "Nick. Nice to meet you."

Jake searched his face a moment. "Hey, don't you work the door at the Hellhole sometimes? I think I've seen you there."

He laughed a little. "Yeah. That's where Gordon met me, actually."

"You one of Gordon's pups?"

The half laugh turned into a choked guffaw. "No. No, I'm nobody's dog."

Jake's eyebrows shot up. "No offense," he said, with just a slight touch of frost in his voice.

Maybe he's somebody's dog.

"No, none taken," Nick said, shaking his head. "Just that it's the same mistake Gordon made. We made it up all right though."

"Glad to hear that," Jake said, "if it means you're joining us tonight."

Jake wasn't his type, but the flirting was nice—if nothing else, it was nice to be wanted—so Nick gave him a crooked smile. "Glad I could join. Anything I should know, being a first-timer?"

Jake's shoulders straightened, and he shifted into good host mode. "The house safeword is just red—keep it simple, you know? We provide condoms and gloves, but no messy play outside the wet room. Respect people's no. Just because someone's on their knees doesn't mean they're free to be used." His mouth quirked. "Unless that's been okayed by prior arrangement, of course. You'll know if that's the case. Otherwise, just feel free to wander around and enjoy. There's snacks and drinks in the kitchen. We do ask that you put some money in the jar there; most guys give twenty dollars."

"Sure." He'd expected as much. It wasn't free to run these house parties, even if from the look of it, Jake—or whoever owned this house—was comfortably off enough.

"The front room is a chill-out room," he went on. "No sex or nudity. The rest of the downstairs is free game. Upstairs"—he motioned to a staircase, cordoned off with a weirdly tacky black velvet rope— "is off limits. Bathroom and wet room are toward the back."

"Thanks," Nick said, trying for another smile. Jake seemed to have lost interest in flirting, though; he might have thought Nick cute at first glance, but the chemistry wasn't there. The doorbell rang again, then, and Nick took the opportunity to escape before it got any more awkward.

He wandered through the hallway, peeking into doorways. In the kitchen, three men were gathered around a kitchen island—no, four, one was on his hands and knees on the floor, serving as a footrest for one of the men perched on a kitchen stool. Nick moved on, weaving toward the back. In what seemed like a living room with all the furniture removed except two massive leather couches, a group of men were watching a tall, muscular blond being expertly bullwhipped by a short, dark man with a thick beard.

Nick passed by the wet room and doubled back toward the front, checking out the rooms on the other side. A spartan-looking office was hosting what seemed like a schoolboy/teacher scene, one man bent over the desk as another caned him and reprimanded him under his breath for some unspecified offense.

Nick's heart was beating rapidly, half with nerves and half with anticipation. He was still half-hard, and the sights around the house hadn't quelled that throbbing need. He wasn't sure what he wanted—only that he wanted.

Then all that want narrowed to a single point and vanished the moment he stepped into the front room.

Jacob Umber wasn't quite the last person Nick expected to see here, but he was certainly on a short list of them. He wasn't in leather, or even in a deniably leather outfit like Nick had put together. The only concession he seemed to have made was to wear a black suit, rather than the grays and browns he usually favored. He sat on a sofa, one leg hooked over his lap, and kneeling at his booted feet was a slender young man wearing a leather harness across his chest.

They weren't doing anything—from the look of their faces, they could have been two friends discussing the weather over a coffee—yet the man, the boy, was at his feet. Looking entirely at home there.

Nick found that he'd frozen, like a deer in the headlights. Several pairs of eyes looked up at him—including Umber's, whose eyebrows raised and whose lips parted as if he were about to speak. To call out Nick's name, maybe. Before he had a chance, Nick turned around and walked out without another word.

He slammed the front door shut behind him. His heart's drumbeat of anticipation had turned into a sick, syncopated thump that thrummed in his gut, in his temples, in his groin. His stomach turned and turned without stopping, and he dashed into an alleyway to dry-heave until it had passed.

He stood up, shakily. *What the fuck?* He almost said it aloud. All right, so seeing Umber there had taken him off guard—it was his stupid crush that had driven him here, so no wonder about that. But to react as if...what? As if Umber were his long-term spouse who he'd just caught cheating? It made no sense.

"Fuck," he said, and groped for his vape, wishing in that moment more than anything for a real cigarette.

*

When Nick woke up, it was with a sense of doom sitting like a brick in the pit of his stomach and a keen wish that his working week did not include Saturdays.

He considered calling in sick. Even PAs took sick days sometimes, surely, and Umber wasn't exactly helpless without him. It wouldn't even have been too much of a lie, the way his stomach was feeling, but he knew it for what it was—gnawing anxiety, not a stomach bug. *Well, maybe I can call in fucking anxious. He knows I've got mental health issues.*

There were a few moments of cursory argument with himself, but Nick knew he wouldn't be calling in sick. Not when it tasted too much like cowardice. Not when it would make Umber think...well, that something had gone wrong, that there was a reason Nick would be avoiding him after their chance meeting last night. That was the last thing Nick wanted. What he wanted—scratch that—

what he could realistically get was for both of them to forget they'd ever seen each other there. And definitely to forget the boy he'd seen kneeling at Umber's feet, in exactly the spot Nick wanted to be.

"He doesn't want you there," he told himself roughly. He dragged himself out of bed and into a cold shower, then choked down a bland breakfast and headed to the gym. There were still three hours to go until he was due to show up for the start of his shift, and he couldn't bear the idea of not filling them with something. Maybe after a good workout, he'd let himself have a hot shower and lunch, and he could put the whole unpleasantness of last night behind him. *One thing's for sure, I'm never going back there.* Not if there was a chance he'd run into Umber again with another boy fawning at his feet.

Nick put himself through a punishing workout, more than he would usually push himself before starting a day's work, but it helped clear his mind a little. After he was done, he let himself stand in the gym's hot shower for almost ten solid minutes. When he emerged, he could face himself in the mirror again. He grabbed a burger on the way to Umber's, and by the time he'd eaten it, he even managed to feel human.

Umber was sitting at his desk writing in his ledger when Nick came in.

"Afternoon," Nick said, maybe a touch gruffer than usual.

"Good afternoon, Mr. Kurosawa."

He sounded normal. That was good. Maybe there was a chance they could both pretend it had never happened. Still, a tension eddied in the air between them, palpable as the dry crackle before a thunderstorm. When Umber pushed his chair away from his desk to face him, Nick's heart leapt into his mouth.

"I wanted to explain something," Umber said.

Fuck. "If this is about last night," he said roughly, "there's no need. Your private life is your own. I don't want to pry."

"Still. I feel like I have to correct any misconceptions."

Nick bit his lip hard and said nothing. He didn't want to hear Umber justify anything, as if there was something wrong with what he did. What they both did, or wanted to do. "I don't have any misconceptions. You were just there to have a good time with your—your—" He couldn't bring himself to finish the sentence.

"The young man you saw is no anything of mine, Mr. Kurosawa," Umber said softly. "Save for a new-met acquaintance. His...partner was in another room."

There was another word Umber had almost chosen. Nick was sure of it. Master, perhaps, or owner. Did he think Nick was too vanilla to understand, even seeing him at a party like that? "Right."

"So, you were not—" He searched for the words. "You weren't interrupting anything. I...had not been to the event in question for some time."

"Well, I won't be going back," Nick said, voice harsher than he'd intended. "So you won't need to worry about running into me. Making things awkward."

"Please, do not stop going on my account; it's no real loss for me not to attend." Umber half turned away then, as if he didn't want to meet Nick's eyes. When he spoke again, there was an odd tone to his voice. "I...I have to admit I wasn't expecting to see you there either, Mr. Kurosawa."

Nick's stomach did an oddly pleasurable flip; his first instinct was to slap the feeling away with a sarcastic rejoinder. "Nothing in my psychological profile to predict it?"

"Oh, I wouldn't say that."

Goddamn it. Why did Umber always know what to say to throw him off balance?

"It's just that I wasn't expecting to see you with that particular crowd."

Something in his tone prickled at Nick's pride. "You don't have a problem with them, why should I?"

"I don't have a problem with them, no, but..." He shook his head. "Never mind. I apologize."

"It's like I said." Nick held up his hands, a helpless gesture. "Your business is your own."

Umber took a step toward him, oddly halting. Nick couldn't tell whether his legs were bothering him, or if something else interrupted the usually smooth rhythm of his movements. Umber tilted his head, looking at Nick as if he presented a puzzle to figure out. "And...that's how you want it to remain?"

The pleasurable flip of his stomach turned to pure anxiety. *Oh fuck. Oh fuck. He knows.* "What do you mean?" His voice came out harsh, almost grating.

"It's...never mind, Mr. Kurosawa." Umber turned away, showing Nick his profile, bland and impassive. "Thank you for hearing me out, even if, as you say, it isn't your business."

He swallowed. "Of course."

That's how you want it to remain?

The question circled around inside his head like a vulture, never quite descending on its target. What the fuck did he mean by it? How was Nick supposed to just go about his day as normal, after Umber had said something like that? He looked away from Umber's profile, feeling hot blood rush to his face. Why would he have said something like that, unless…

Unless there's something he wants to change.

"Mr. Umber—" he started, then realized he had no idea what he was going to say next.

Umber turned back, Nick still looking down, not meeting his eyes. "What is it, Mr. Kurosawa?"

Would you like me to kneel for you, the way that boy did?

The words were there, but Nick would have rather peeled his own skin off than speak them aloud. Yet he couldn't say what he knew he needed to, couldn't simply say never mind, and get on with the workday. He stood there gawping at the ground, his mouth working soundlessly, wishing abjectly that someone would put him out of his misery.

A moment later, Umber finally did. "I could use your assistance today with a small errand," he said, as if Nick hadn't spoken at all. There was a terrible compassion in his voice that made Nick want to burrow right into the center of the Earth. "I have a few parts on order at a store called Hansen Microtronics, near North Peak Station. If you could pick them up and pay for them?" He took an envelope out of his jacket pocket and proffered it to Nick.

Nick reached out to grab the envelope. For a brief moment, their fingers brushed. It sent a hot current right to the base of Nick's spine. He heard Umber draw a sudden, hitching breath and knew with the certainty of instinct Umber had felt the same.

He wants me. The thought was inescapable. Their eyes met. If they had been in another place—a club, a back alley, a half-deserted beach—Nick would have known what to do. Would have closed the distance between them, or gone to his knees, offering himself without a shred of shame. If Umber had been another man, maybe he would have done it in the store, right there and then.

Nick took a slow, deliberate step back, keeping eye contact with Umber, and slid the envelope into his jacket pocket. Umber's face was hard to read—it always was—but his eyebrows twitched slightly, and Nick heard the click of his teeth snapping together.

"Of course," Nick said, his fingers still tingling. "Would you like me to bring them back to the store, or—?"

"Home, please," Umber said.

Of course. He didn't have a computer at the store, only in his home office—that tricked-out battle station that would have seemed more at home in a rich teenager's bedroom. "I'll see you there, Mr. Umber," he said, and walked out of the store without waiting to see if Umber responded.

He decided to walk a few blocks to clear his head, but it wasn't getting clear. All he could think of was the moment they had touched, and some of Umber's armor had fallen away—that, and what he had said. The way he had said it.

That's how you want it to remain?

How was he supposed to tell Umber that what he wanted most of all was to trade places with that damn kid and go on his knees awaiting Umber's command? It was an almost physical need, something deeper down than lust. No matter what had passed between them, that couldn't be what Umber wanted too. Even if it was, would he even allow himself to want it? Nick was his assistant, after all. He snorted a humorless laugh. His hired gun.

Another block managed to get him clearheaded enough that he could put thoughts of Umber—all thoughts—out of his head for a moment. He fell into a rhythmic stride, the easy gait of someone who knew he might have miles more to go before he could rest, and let his legs and his instinct guide the way. He was walking parallel to the subway line; he could have doubled back at this point and gotten on at Starling Station, but he liked being out in the fresh air. He could take an Uber back, or the subway. Some part of him felt a vague twinge of guilt at using up his time on the clock walking off the mess in his head, but he ignored it. Better to take the time to think clearly so that he wasn't going to do anything stupid when he went back to Umber's apartment.

When he picked up the parts, he made the decision to get an Uber. The box was the size of a widescreen TV, and heavy. Taking that on the subway would have been foolish. He sat in the back with the box under his arm, watching the light over the city grow dim with the coming night. On the way up to Umber's penthouse, he saw his reflections in the elevator surrounding him, identical men carrying identical boxes, their faces shuttered and unreadable.

Umber was already at home, waiting in his office.

"I've got the parts," Nick said. "Where would you like me to put them?"

"In the closet, please."

The office must have been meant as a bedroom. The closet was almost as big as Umber's walk-in, filled with about twenty computers in various states of disassembly, as well as several more monitors, printers of every shape and size, and something Nick was pretty sure was an older model of 3D printer. He put the box down. Umber was typing on his beast of a mechanical keyboard, the clicking of it burrowing into the back of Nick's brain. He realized he was angry at Umber—had been angry for a few hours now. He knew it was stupid, that he had no right to be angry at Umber, but it was there nonetheless. The way he had dangled his lure and then withdrew it. That wasn't fair of him. Nick clenched and unclenched his fists, standing near the closet door.

Then he turned around. "What did you mean?"

Umber stopped typing and turned his chair around. "Excuse me?"

"Earlier today." Nick forced his breathing into a calmer rhythm, but he had to say something—had to, if the anger weren't to curdle into something worse. If he got fired, he got fired, he thought, with reckless, fatalistic humor. "You asked me—"

"Mr. Kurosawa—"

"Let me finish."

Umber's silence made it harder to continue. Nick forced himself to meet his eyes.

"You asked me if this was how I wanted things to remain. Not...being involved in your private life. What did you mean?"

Umber was quiet another long moment, then he looked away. "I should not have said that."

"But you did. And I want—I'd like to know what you meant."

"Mr. Kurosawa, I did not intend to make you uncomfortable, in the slightest. It was unfair for me to say that and, as your employer, frankly inappropriate, and I— I unreservedly apologize. I can only hope I have not damaged our working relationship."

The words had all rushed out at once, one of the longest uninterrupted sentences Umber had ever spoken. The skin over his cheekbones was blotched with red, and his eyes darted left and right as if he—

As if he feels trapped.

"You didn't...harass me, or anything," Nick said, his voice low.

"Still." Umber turned away. "I crossed a line."

"What if I wanted you to cross it?"

Umber laughed, then cut it short abruptly, still not facing him. "It doesn't make it right. I—I've tried to distract myself, but..." He heaved a sigh. "The point is that what I want from you is not something I can ever ask for, Mr. Kurosawa."

Nick's heart was jackhammering in his chest; his fingertips tingled with heat. In an instant, he understood Umber's halting attempts at explanation. It had been nerves. He'd been looking for distraction at the play party, too, hadn't he? Distraction from me, Nick thought, almost not daring to.

He took a step forward, licking his lips. "What if I were to offer?"

*

Umber looked at him, his expression carefully blank. "What are you offering?"

Nick's face went hot. When he spoke again it was in a low, fierce tone. "You know what I'm offering, sir."

"I'm not your sir," he said, then snorted a sudden, unexpected laugh. Not a mocking one—it was oddly defensive. "I'm—I'm not asking you to get on your knees."

Nick grinned with clenched teeth. "Would you like me to?"

He breathed out sharply. "Is this a game for you?"

"No." Nick swallowed. "It isn't a game."

"So tell me. What are you offering?"

"My service. My—" His breath hitched. "My obedience. However you want it."

Umber held his gaze for a moment, then looked away. "I'm your employer, Mr. Kurosawa. I couldn't possibly accept."

"You only pay me for some of my time," Nick said. "The rest of it is mine."

"That's sophistry."

He swallowed. "So fire me."

Umber looked back at him, and for the first time, Nick saw something like shock in his sea-glass eyes. "Fire you? Mr. Kurosawa—"

"I—I want this, all right? I want you. If I need to go back to doorman work for you to even consider it..." He laughed hollowly; he knew he sounded desperate, and couldn't bring himself to care.

Umber was silent for a while. "All right."

The breath caught in Nick's throat. He realized he hadn't actually expected Umber to take his offer—that he'd expected to be back in his shitty apartment before sunset. "All right?"

"You heard what I said. But...you are too valuable for me to lose your skills. So, during your work hours, things continue as they have. Those are the boundaries. If you choose to stay after they are over, I will take what you are offering. Your service. Your obedience. However I choose it."

It was about the longest speech Umber had ever made.

"However you choose it," Nick echoed, not sure if he was agreeing, or asking a question. *What do you want, what are you into, what about a safeword.* He knew he should ask the question, but somehow the words didn't come to him. His mouth was dry and sticky as if he'd gone a long, hot day without water. He swallowed.

"Tell me what you're thinking, Nick." It was the first time Umber had said his first name. No more Mr. Kurosawa.

He forced himself to speak. "What about a safeword?" It was the only thing he could get out.

Umber cocked his head, looking at him. "No," he said after a while, "that won't be necessary. I don't want to play games of resistance with you, Nick. Your no will always be respected."

"What if—what if I say no just to provoke you?"

"That would be...disappointing."

A shiver crawled down Nick's spine and settled in his lower belly. "Would you punish me?"

Umber smiled a little. "If you feel that you need punishment, Nick, I would be more than happy to oblige. But you offered me your service, not your defiance."

Umber closed the distance between them and reached to adjust the collar of Nick's shirt. It was a startlingly proprietary gesture. Nick made himself hold still beneath it.

"I expect you to serve to the best of your ability. And I prefer positive reinforcement over negative. Any good teacher..." He caught Nick's eye, and for the first time there was a glint of mischief in his gray-green eyes. "Any good teacher, or any good animal trainer, would tell you the same."

Then he slapped Nick, full in the face. It was not hard, exactly, but it was precise, expertly judged. Nick gasped, a flood of warmth rushing to his face, and between his legs.

Umber's face was sober now, the glint of mischief gone. "That was because I could," he said, "and because I knew you would enjoy it. You do not have to misbehave to get things you enjoy, Nick."

Nick only stood there, breathing hard, any thoughts wiped out of him. He couldn't quite tell what he was feeling—only that he wanted more of it.

Umber took a step back, breaking the touch between them. "Hm. I can see that you need some time to process this. Go and run a bath for me, and come back to get me when it's done."

Nick started moving before he'd quite processed what Umber had said, his legs carrying him to the bathroom on autopilot. He knelt and started the tap running. Within a few moments, silky gray steam filled the room. He threw in two handfuls of Epsom salts and added a few drops of lavender oil, then the hypoallergenic bath soap, stirring it until the suds were thick as meringue.

Finally, he stood up. He realized that sometime in the last few moments, his heart had stopped beating double time. He was breathing deeply, evenly—somehow, he had become something like calm.

He closed his eyes for just a moment, oddly aware of his own body—not any particular part of it, but the totality of it, of his own presence in space. He opened his eyes and walked out of the bathroom to get Umber. Every step he took seemed to be graceful and deliberate; it was almost the opposite of being drunk, with everything sharpened and in technicolor clarity.

When he entered, Umber was sitting on the sofa, his hands in his lap, looking into the middle distance. Nick cleared his throat.

"Your bath is ready, Mr. Umber."

Somehow, he knew it was the right thing, to use his name, not to say sir. Umber started to rise, but before he could get to his feet, Nick was standing beside him, offering his arm. Umber glanced up at him and smiled: thin, closed-mouthed, but so genuine it made Nick's heart leap into his throat.

"Thank you, Nick."

He walked him to the bathroom. He wondered if Umber would ask him to come in—to wash him, perhaps—but he halted Nick at the bathroom door.

"In my wardrobe," Umber said, "there is a white terry cloth robe. I would like you to bring it down now. Then I would like you to wait for me, here, while I bathe."

Nick inclined his head and went toward Umber's bedroom. When he was about halfway to the door, he heard the click of the bathroom door locking behind Umber. For a moment, he felt a twinge of disappointment, but it almost didn't register—he was still carried on the back of that strange, calm grace.

By the time he came back to the bathroom door with the terry cloth robe, he realized it was something like happiness.

*

Nick knocked gently at the door. "I've got your robe, Mr. Umber."

There was no answer from inside, only a slosh of water. Well, Umber had told him to wait, so he'd wait. He held the robe folded over his arm and stood at ease, legs slightly apart, and let his eyes go ever so slightly unfocused. Thoughts were starting to come back to him, after that brief, almost blissful period where he had moved and acted without the constant noise that buzzed in his head. They fell over one another like badly arranged dominoes. *What am I doing? Do I look stupid? Why did he lock me out of the bathroom? Doesn't he want to fuck me? Will he want me to fuck him?*

He flexed his hands around the terry cloth robe. This is for him, he reminded himself. Umber had asked him to stand here and hold it. He'd given him his orders. Nothing else mattered. For a while, he could almost believe that.

The lock clicked open; he took a quick, harsh breath. Umber opened the door. He was wrapped in a towel from the waist down. It was the first time Nick had seen this much of him. His shoulders, with their surprising heft of muscle on Umber's small frame, were covered with dewdrops of water. His chest was barrel-shaped, scarred, dusted with brown hair. There was a little swell of a belly, a middle-aged paunch, and then the white edge of a towel at the curve of his hip. Nick's breath caught in his throat; he wanted nothing more than to trail his lips down to that towel and nuzzle beneath it.

He swallowed and held the robe out, helping Umber step into it as if it were his tweed coat.

Umber tied the robe tightly and looked up at him. "You are sure about this?" The words came slowly, almost reluctantly, and Nick's heart was beating so hard he thought it'd fly out of his chest. This wasn't some academic exercise for Umber, no matter how cool he might seem on the surface; there was desire in his eyes, raw and real. Desire for him. "There are still...ethical implications to what we are doing. With you as my employee."

"I'll quit if you want." The words came out rough, husky. "I've told you that."

"I don't want you to quit." Umber's voice was soft. "As I said, I've—I've rather come to rely on you, Mr. Kurosawa."

Mr. Kurosawa, again, Nick noted. It twisted at something inside him, pulling in two directions, the tenderness and the formality of it both.

It's what he calls me when we're speaking as equals.

"But," Umber said, "I am afraid I have let myself...indulge something I shouldn't have."

He swallowed, reached up a hand, and laid it against Nick's cheek. Nick leaned into the touch with a soft moan—it was the perfect, tender echo of Umber's slap.

"I want this," Nick said. "I'm walking into this with my eyes open."

"There are always considerations we cannot see, Mr. Kurosawa."

"So tell me to leave. I'll leave."

Umber drew back his hand.

"Or tell me to quit. Or, just..." He licked his lips and took a chance. He went to his knees, took the hand that had both hurt and caressed him between both of his, and pressed his mouth to Umber's knuckles.

Umber breathed in sharply, and Nick felt him almost—almost—withdraw the hand from his touch.

Nick held on to it loosely for another moment, then let go, but his mouth was still nuzzled against it. "You said," he murmured against Umber's skin. "You said 'all right,' you said we could do this." He knew how childish he sounded, how petulant, but he didn't care.

"Nick."

The sound of his name went through him like a bullet.

"Stand up."

He stood, straightening his back.

"What do you want, Nick?"

Umber's voice was soft, but it hit Nick like a blow; he gritted his teeth, not wanting to answer. *I want to be useful, used, yours.* He couldn't quite say it. *I want to be your property.*

"Nick, look at me."

Slowly, he raised his head, meeting the eyes of the shorter man standing before him. Umber wasn't quite smiling, but he looked pleased nonetheless, as if Nick had performed some difficult task to his specifications, rather than just looked him in the eyes.

"Would you like me to hurt you?"

A soft groan escaped Nick's lips, involuntarily. Umber's hand came to rest on his chest, rubbing small circles on his breastbone, the way one might soothe a nervous animal. He didn't break eye contact the entire time.

Nick swallowed and squared his shoulders, forcing himself to hold Umber's gaze. Swimming in gray-green. "I just want to please you."

"That's not good enough, Nick."

God. Nick had been whipped, paddled, kicked around. He'd been used by rough-handed men who didn't care much for his pleasure. He'd been shouted at by drill instructors, called every degrading name under the sun. But nobody had been as wonderfully, exactingly cruel to him as Jacob Umber was being right now.

"If you want to please me," he said, "you'll tell me what you want, right now."

Nick was breathing hard. Somewhere, distantly, he knew his cock was hard too, but it seemed the least important thing in the room at the moment. The place where Umber was touching him burned with an electric current. "I—I want to—" His hands were making fists at his sides, coiling and uncoiling. Umber only looked at him, terribly patient. "I want to kneel for you."

It was the closest he could come to articulating that ache to be owned. Umber seemed to accept it. He stepped back, breaking eye contact, lifting his hand off of Nick's chest. "Very good," he said, and hearing that nearly brought Nick to his knees again right then. "And you will. But not right now."

For a moment, they were both silent, Nick's breathing slowly returning to normal. "Thank you," he said finally, in something barely more than a whisper.

"You're very welcome." There was a deep sincerity in Umber's voice that was hard to listen to.

"So." He swallowed. "We're trying this."

"We're trying this," Umber echoed and reached up to stroke his cheek again. "But not tonight. I...tried to go too fast with you, and I am sorry for that."

Nick laughed. "This isn't exactly what I'm used to. Taking it slow."

"I'm not interested in rushing anything," Umber said, and the way he spoke made it sound like foreplay, like a promise, like everything Nick wanted.

And now, Umber was going to make him wait.

"Go home, Mr. Kurosawa. I will see you tomorrow, as usual. Tomorrow night..." He smiled with one side of his mouth. "Tomorrow night, we can try."

Nick let out a shuddering breath. "Sure you don't want me to stay?"

"I've told you what I want, Nick."

He closed his eyes a moment. When he opened them again, he nodded. "Good night, Mr. Umber."

"Good night, Nick. I—I look forward to tomorrow."
Me too. God, me too.

*

Nick thought he wouldn't be able to sleep at all, after being sent home from Umber's apartment, but the moment his head hit the pillow, he fell into dreamless slumber. He woke up almost exactly seven hours later, an hour before his alarm, and felt more rested than he had in a long while.

He swung his feet out of bed and pulled the curtain open. The sky was very blue, the sun low and bright. There was a tingle at his breastbone, right where Umber had touched him last night, and raised his hand to press his fingers to his bare chest.

Well. That had really happened, hadn't it?

The cold linoleum of the floor chilled his feet. He'd left his phone charging on the bookshelf in the living room and picked it up to check his notifications. There was an e-mail from Umber. The subject was "Regarding last night's conversation." Nick's heart caught in his throat. *He'll go back on what he said. He'll fire me. He'll never want to see me again.*

He slammed the phone facedown on the dining table, hard enough that he winced—*fuck, I hope I haven't broken it. Stupid, Kurosawa.* Still, he left it there without picking it up and checking he hadn't cracked the screen, and went to make himself a coffee. Everything was easier to face with a cup of coffee in him.

He made it strong, half a cup full, and topped the rest up with cold water from the tap so he could gulp it down. He regretted it instantly. Sour heartburn flared up, and he had to drink another mug full of cold water to calm it down. He made another cup, vowing to drink it more slowly this time, and grabbed a cereal bar from the cupboard before sitting down at the dining table.

He turned over his phone. *Well, at least it's not cracked.* With a shuddering breath he unlocked it and opened up the e-mail from Umber.

It wasn't what he'd expected.

It had been sent at four in the morning. There wasn't any salutation. He wondered if Umber hadn't known whether to call him "Nick" or "Mr. Kurosawa." It went straight to the point.

> If you have any regrets about what passed between us, please do not feel any sort of obligation to continue on this path. I know you are a man of your word, but consider this leave to back out graciously. If you also wish to quit your position as my PA, I will provide severance, and connect you with an acquaintance in San Francisco who may be able to find you work.

Nick blinked. He was almost insulted. What had he done for Umber to think he was already looking for an exit route? He'd practically served himself up on a silver platter!

The e-mail went on. Nick shifted his shoulders.

> While I generally trust my instincts, there are lines you may not want crossed, lines that may be invisible to me. I meant what I said about not being interested in playing with your resistance, and that your right to say no will always be respected, without question. For clarity's sake, though, I want those lines laid out.

Something I will require of you above all else is honesty. You needn't lay yourself open, but when I ask a question regarding what you want, or what you do not want, I cannot accept less than that.

Because I am asking it of you, I will show you the same consideration. I will tell you what I want, and what lines I require you not to cross. It is up to you whether you want to have these conversations face to face, or through letters.

Letters, he wrote. Nick almost rolled his eyes. Not "e-mails," which was what they were damn well doing.

I am not looking for you to fill out a checklist, only to have an honest conversation about our needs and our desires. One of which, of course, is possibly to end this before it begins. I must admit, though, that I hope that is not what you want.

Please write back soon, and let me know.

He hadn't signed it. Nick read it again, then once more for a third time. By that point, he'd finished off his second cup of coffee and the cereal bar.

It seemed so cool, on the surface, so controlled. Written with perfect grammar and punctuation, even with a time stamp closer to sunrise than sunset. It had taken him three reads to see the cracks in the facade. Umber's version of the desperate late-night text. The justifications, the multiple outs he offered, the final "please" in his last line. He was just as worried as Nick.

He made his third coffee of the morning, popped some bread in the toaster, then hit Reply and started writing.

> Let's do it this way. Probably easier for me to get my thoughts out.
>
> Usually any negotiation I've done has been quick and dirty, and in the moment. So this is new to me. I'll try to be as honest as I can.

Nick took a shuddery breath before he continued, thumb moving across the phone's keyboard.

> What I know I want is to be in your control, and to please you. And yeah, I like pain. I like to be flogged and caned and slapped. I like enduring it. I like the way it makes me feel. But it's not as important as feeling—

Nick cut the sentence off there. He wanted to write: "not as important as feeling like I'm yours." But that was a hell of a heavy thing to write in something that, in essence, was like working out where to have your first date.

He grimaced. They'd gone a little past first dates, surely. This thing, this connection they'd forged, fragile as it was, might have been new, but he'd known Umber for months now. Had learned the rhythm of his life. Still—no. Umber might have asked for honesty, but he'd also said Nick didn't need to lay himself entirely open. It was too much, too fast. Instead, he wrote:

> But it's not as important as feeling under your control.

After a moment's thought, he added another few sentences.

> Usually I fuck guys I play with, or they fuck me, but I know some people like to keep fucking and kink separate. I don't know how you do it, yet. I'd like to know.

He realized, reading it over, that he'd dodged asking any direct questions. So had Umber, for that matter. They were still dancing around each other. It hadn't been this tentative, this fraught, last night—it had felt so completely natural. Nick sighed and ran a hand through his hair. It stood up on end in jagged directions. He hit Send and went to take a shower.

When he'd finished his shower, he'd already gotten a reply. He swore under his breath. "Do you ever sleep?"

> I am glad you want to feel under my control. I want you under it.

"Fuck," Nick said softly. He bit his lip.

> I enjoy compelling your obedience, and using your service; I will enjoy watching you react to receiving pain.

Jacob Umber was possibly the only man Nick had ever known who'd use a semicolon in his sexts. *Is this sexting?* Whatever it was, it knocked the breath out of him and stirred his cock to half-hardness.

> I generally prefer to use my hands over using any other implements, but I will keep in mind you enjoy being caned and flogged.

All right, in Nick's book this definitely counted as sexting. He let out a soft, whimpery moan and let his hand drift to the growing bulge in his boxer shorts.

> As for sexual service, I may ask it of you in the future, knowing you wouldn't be averse. However, it is not what drives me. I do not think it is what drives you either.

He wasn't wrong about that, but right at that moment, Nick wasn't being driven by much more. He rubbed at his cock through the fabric of his boxers, hearing Umber's voice purr in the back of his mind. *I want you under my control. I will use my hands on you, Nick, would you like that? Would you like to service me, Nick?*

"Fuck," he said again, this time with more emphasis. His cock was rock-hard now, and precome was making a wet circle at the front of his boxers. He stroked himself through it, not allowing himself the pleasure of skin on skin. He read the message again, hearing every word in Umber's soft and precise voice, skimming his palm over the heated length of his cock. He imagined kneeling in front of him, needy and desperate, pressing his lips to Umber's hands. He thought of taking his broad, nimble fingers into his mouth, sucking them one by one, hearing Umber's breath hitch in his throat, feeling the thrum of his pulse beneath his tongue as he kissed his wrist...

Something made him pull away. He breathed shakily, trying to regain some sort of composure. His cock jutted out like a tent pole, jumping with frustrated need. He groaned softly. *What am I doing to myself?*

Nick knew it instantly. *I don't want to come without his hands on me.*

After long minutes of trying to get himself under control, he was still half-hard, and that probably wouldn't go away without a cold shower. *Cold shower it is, then.* He stripped off his boxers. He reeked of sex and sweat, despite barely exerting himself.

He stood under the cool stream of water until his dick finally agreed to listen to him and the last of his hard-on subsided. He half expected to have that awful, wrenching feeling of blue balls, but instead, there was only a kind of gathered tension in his solar plexus.

After he'd dressed, his clothes seemed too tight on him; his hands prickled. He still remembered, with vivid, full-sensory clarity, the way it had felt when Umber slapped his cheek. So precise, so well-judged. There wasn't a trace of it in the mirror, which Nick almost regretted. He wondered if Umber would leave marks, once they got past this awkward negotiation. Once he'd given himself free rein.

Nick breathed out sharply. *You're supposed to calm down, Kurosawa.* The last thing he needed was for his treacherous cock to rise again, tenting his trousers throughout his whole workday. God—he was meant to get through a day of assisting Mr. Umber with his ordinary needs before the doors of his penthouse shut behind them and he could...

Well. What he could do still remained to be seen. All that remained was to get through the day without all the blood rushing out of his head and leaving him flat-out in a faint with the world's most raging hard-on.

He snorted. *I'm not a teenager anymore. I can get through one day without coming in my pants.*

*

It was, to Nick's surprise, actually easy to get through the day as if it were normal. When he walked into the store and greeted Umber with his usual tone of voice, and asked if he wanted his coffee now, it just seemed, well, normal. He was doing his job; he was busy. Even when Umber called him to his desk, he only felt a kind of curiosity, not the thrumming anxiety he'd half expected.

"I am considering the purchase of a car," Umber said. "Now that I have a reliable driver available, it may be more convenient than renting a car when it's required."

"So how can I help?"

He smiled up at Nick—there was a moment where that anxiety buzzed to the surface, but it was almost pleasant, and oddly distant. Nick realized, then, he wasn't anxious, not really. He was anticipating. "I would like you to research some of the possible options and bring them to me."

"What kind of options are you looking at?"

"I'll leave that in your hands, Mr. Kurosawa. What I require is a vehicle that is capable of longer journeys, is not too ostentatious, and has...a good suite of safety features."

Nick smiled crookedly. "Something you might drive a president in."

Umber raised an eyebrow. "If you will."

"What's the budget I'm looking at?"

"Keep it reasonable," Umber said mildly. "I am not looking to purchase a...a supercar."

"Got it—no Porsche Spyder. Even if it would suit you." It was as if something had loosened in him—he could joke with Umber, suddenly, he could relax around him. Knowing that when they were back in his apartment Umber could do whatever he wanted with him was oddly, paradoxically, freeing. "When are you looking to have this car?"

"I'd like a list of options by tomorrow evening, please."

"Would help if you had a computer in here to do the research."

He raised an eyebrow again, and the corner of his mouth turned up in a quirk of a smile. "You're resourceful, Mr. Kurosawa. You'll find a way to do the necessary research."

He suppressed his own smile. "Of course, Mr. Umber. Anything else?"

Umber held his eyes for a moment. Warmth prickled between them, the foreknowledge of later. The memory of the night before. "That will be all, Mr. Kurosawa. For now."

Nick's stomach clenched with the unspoken promise in those two words, and he felt a rush of heat between his legs—but he merely inclined his head and went to work. He was on the clock, after all.

A few hours later, and a few dealerships called, both in Westerley and surrounding cities, Nick had secured a decent list of options, with the assurance several catalogues would be arriving at Umber's store tomorrow, rushed overnight. Two of the dealerships had offered to take him on test drives that day, but he demurred despite their incentives. Interesting, how eager to please people were when they thought you were rich.

He'd also picked up lunch for Umber, and closed up the shop after Umber had gone home early. He stood up and stretched. Ordinarily, on days where Umber went home early, Nick would wait for a call to see if he was needed. Sometimes, Umber wanted some privacy, and he never seemed to bother tallying up Nick's hours. His phone was heavy in his pocket. What would he do if Umber didn't call? Go over there anyway? Present himself at the door, ready for...

"For whatever he wants," Nick murmured aloud. A bolt of dark heat went through him, curling like a wild beast in his belly.

When his phone buzzed, he nearly jumped out of his skin. He got it out of his pocket so rapidly he almost dropped it on the floor.

Would you like to come join me at my apartment, Nick?

The coiled heat became a blaze; his heartbeat pulsed in his lips. *Yes, God, finally.* Only then did Nick let himself give in fully to the anticipation that had been shading the entirety of his day. He made his way to Clarebrook Towers with a speed that seemed almost supernatural—not a rush, just a gliding grace that carried him as if he were on oiled rails. Everything seemed new, somehow, the lobby's lights sparkling on the tiles, the penthouse elevator gleaming. He knew what it was. Some haze that had been over his eyes had fallen away. The world seemed crisper, more colorful because he was paying more attention.

He punched the code into Umber's door and entered. Soft music was playing, some classical composition Nick didn't recognize—not that he'd recognize many of them. Umber wasn't in the living room. "Hello?" Nick called out.

"In here, please." Umber's voice came from the office.

Nick's heart was suddenly in his throat. He walked into the office. Umber stood by the desk, the monitors off. His jacket hung over the back of his chair, and he had undone his cuff links and laid them on the desktop. They shone like small dull stars under the overhead light. He was slowly, methodically rolling up his sleeves.

"Do you know," he said, his voice oddly conversational, "that I am notified whenever someone accesses the penthouse elevator?"

Nick swallowed.

"Answer me when I ask a question, please."

"No," Nick said, his mouth dry. He could not keep his eyes off Umber rolling up his sleeves. His forearms weren't as muscular as his shoulders; there was a lean grace to them. "But I could have guessed."

"Now you know for sure." He finished rolling up his sleeves. "Please come to the desk."

Nick went. There was no question of not going—Umber's soft "please" was more compelling than any man's bluster and command had been, before.

"Bend over slightly. Put your hands down flat on the desktop."

He did. His index finger brushed against the cool metal of Umber's cuff links. Behind him, he heard the rustle of Umber taking off his belt.

"Let me make something very clear, Nick," Umber whispered, his breath warm against the curve of Nick's ear. "I am not doing this to punish you. I am doing this because I think we will both enjoy it—and because I want to see how you react to it. Do you understand me?"

"Yes, Mr. Umber."

"Good. Stay still, Nick." He pressed his hand to Nick's ass, not cupping it as much as just resting his hand against its curve. Even through his trousers, Nick felt how hot Umber's hand was. When he withdrew it, Nick let out a breathy little moan of need. "Let us begin."

*

When his belt came down, Nick gasped—not in pain, it hadn't hurt, but despite expecting it, the slap of leather on fabric had startled him. He braced himself against the desk a little better, spreading his legs for balance, and to give Umber better access to his ass. He warmed Nick up slowly, excruciatingly slowly, starting with deliberately paced strokes that barely did more than letting him know the belt was there. He wanted to squirm, to beg for more—but Umber had told him to stay, so he stayed, silent and shivering. When Umber started putting more force into his strokes, Nick groaned, arching himself to catch more of it.

"That's very good, Nick," he said after ten more strokes, and stopped.

Nick shuddered involuntarily. His hands were still flat on the desk, but his finger had curled over one of the cuff links; he was holding onto it like a talisman.

"I'd like you to take your trousers off now."

Nick cleared his throat. "May—may I remove my hands from the desk?"

"You may." There was unalloyed pleasure in Umber's voice.

He liked that I asked. It made something warm spread in Nick's chest. He stood up slowly, all too aware of Umber standing behind him, belt in hand, and undid his own belt. The leather was soft, almost slick, under his fingertips.

"Do you want me to...take off my underpants too?"

"Trousers only, Nick."

He folded the trousers—somehow, he thought that was what Umber would want—and put them on the desk chair, then reassumed his position, hands splayed on the desktop, bent low so his ass presented an easy target. He felt more naked than if he'd just been able to take his underpants off, and his shirt. His socks were still on, he noticed, with something like amusement. *Well, he didn't ask me to take my socks off.*

The first strike of the belt came harder, this time, as if Umber had judged how much he could take and adjusted accordingly. It drove the breath out of Nick, and his fingers curled against the smooth wood of the desk. In the matte black monitors, he saw their shadowy reflections, washed of all color: one man bent over, the other standing behind and slightly to the side.

The belt came down five, ten, twenty more times; then, he lost count. Endless licks of fire warmed him, burned him. With every stroke he made a soft, helpless noise, half gasp and half moan, and arched his back, begging wordlessly for more, for mercy, for Umber's touch.

Nick had taken harder strokes before, but it wasn't the pain that made it feel so—intense, so right, so hard to bear and wonderful all at once. It was that he had promised to stand still for it, that he could end it all just by saying no, by saying stop, but he chose to stand there and take whatever Umber could give him. No matter how long he went on.

"Nick." Umber's voice seemed to be coming from very far away. It cut through the haze nonetheless, like a candle in a fog. "I want you to tell me how you are feeling."

For a moment, Nick just blinked, uncomprehending. How could he want words from him, right now? His hands clenched; his finger brushed Umber's cuff link again, cool and solid. He closed his eyes. "I feel," he said, his voice thick, "far. Like I'm floating, a little. But good."

Umber laid the belt down and moved closer, the warmth of his body against Nick's side, his hand on the back of Nick's neck. "Come back to me now," he said. "You have done very well. You have pleased me very well, Nick."

Nick sagged a little, his hands almost giving out, then straightened a little, pushing himself up close against Umber. "Just by...just by taking a belting?"

Umber's hand tightened slightly on his neck, as if he were about to squeeze. "There is no just about it. When I praise you, Nick, I expect you not to argue with me about it."

Nick screwed his eyes shut tight. "I'm sorry," he whispered.

"There is no need. I had not yet expressed my wishes on the matter. Now I have—now you know. Isn't that right?"

"Yes. Now I know."

"So I will say it again. You have pleased me, Nick."

He knew what to say now. "Thank you." His eyes were still shut, so tight he could see lights dancing behind them.

Umber drew back, just a little. Nick felt the absence of him, a sudden, yawning void. He wanted to burrow himself against Umber, to lay skin against skin, to feel his warmth.

"Put your trousers back on, Nick, and come into the living room when you've had a chance to settle yourself." He left him then, Nick still splayed spread-eagled against the desk.

Put his trousers back on? Nick blinked in confusion down at the desktop. He wasn't going to fuck him—wasn't going to do anything more than an over-the-underwear spanking?

Well. Nick grinned at his dark reflection in the monitor. He did say he liked to take things slowly. It wasn't the end. It was the promise of more to come. It had to be. Even if more wasn't going to come tonight.

Nick put his trousers on. He had to take a few deep breaths before he could walk into the living room and face Umber. He was there, pouring two glasses of water from a massive pitcher filled with ice and lemons. Nick felt an errant stab of guilt. *I should have been the one to prepare that.*

Umber handed him the glass. He drank deeply, greedily. He hadn't been aware of how parched he'd been until then.

"How are you feeling now?"

Nick took another sip and assessed himself. His heart was still pounding heavily, and his ass ached slightly; he was horny, and exhausted. Over and above that, though, there was something else, two other things, in fact. He felt grounded, contented—that was one. As for the other, he wanted to lay his head in Umber's lap and sleep there, satisfied as a cat. He tried to find a way to sum it up, and finally settled on "Good. I feel good." He blinked slowly, like a man coming out of a daze. "Do you need anything, Mr. Umber?"

Umber smiled at him. It was a fond smile, and it suited his face more than any Nick had seen before. "Not at this moment, Nick, thank you. Please, sit down."

He hadn't gestured to either the sofa or the love seat. Instinctively, Nick sat on the floor, by the sofa, and leaned against it.

Umber sat on the sofa and gingerly put a hand on Nick's shoulder. It wasn't quite what Nick craved, but it was good—God, it was good. He leaned his head against Umber's touch and let out a long, satisfied sigh.

"You know, you didn't have to do that," Umber said. "Sit on the floor."

"I know," Nick said softly. He turned his head slightly to look at Umber. "Is it all right that I wanted to?"

"Of course it's all right." Umber frowned slightly. "It is always all right to want, Nick. Who told you that it wasn't?"

"Nobody." He made a noise that could have been a laugh. "Everybody."

Umber went quiet after that, not reaching out for him nor moving his hand, just letting him lean there.

"Thank you," Nick said after a while, his voice so soft it was almost a whisper.

Umber pressed his leg hard against Nick's side, a comforting pressure. "Please don't think I do this solely for your benefit." There was a thin thread of amusement in his voice, so very him that Nick smiled to himself.

"I know," he said again. "But. Thank you anyway. For...trusting that I want this. For trying something."

"Hm." It was a low, satisfied kind of sound; it went through Nick. "Let's not be thanking each other yet. It makes me think of something ending. And I would like to think this is merely beginning."

Nick hugged his knees and hid his face in his arms so Umber wouldn't see his grin. "Yeah," he said. "Me too."

Part Three

CHANGES

A part of Nick, he slowly realized, hadn't expected things to last, at least not more than a week.

A week had always been the outer limits of his relationships, loosely defined. Either they would shade into friendship, like with Alex, or vanish into thin air, like with Kirby, or the dozen others who'd left their—literal and figurative—marks on him. Umber would get tired of him. Maybe Nick would lose his job along with whatever had burned between them. He would have accepted that. He'd judged it worth the risk.

When the week came and went and Umber kept calling him back to his apartment—when another week followed, and another, and he'd been bent over desk, leather sofa, kitchen island—when Umber showed no sign at all of tiring of Nick's company...something loosened in him. Some knot of tension in his heart that had been part of him for years relaxed, just a little, and he stopped waiting for the other shoe to drop.

Umber was at home today; he'd judged his energy too low to head out to the shop, so Nick was manning it. Strictly, it wasn't a PA duty, but Nick had fallen into it easily enough on those days when Umber required it. It wasn't easy, as it kept him busy when Umber needed silence and solitude to manage his pain. "If all goes well,"

Umber had said on the phone that morning, "I may still be able to receive your visit tonight."

Nick hoped, very much, that all would go well.

His phone buzzed in his pocket, and he fished it out. An e-mail had come in from Umber—the subject line read "Nick." His heart leapt into his throat.

> Before you come to me, I would like you to stop at the grocery store on Whyte Avenue and pick up ingredients for a meal that you can prepare, using the card I gave you. I want you to cook for us tonight, and I'd like to be surprised.

Nick's heart remained lodged in his throat, now half with nerves rather than with anticipation. He had the feeling this was, somehow, a test—maybe not one he could fail, per se, but a test nonetheless. A meal you can prepare... There was a hell of a backhanded insult hidden in that. Nick snorted a laugh. Was Umber expecting cup ramen and cut-up hot dogs? Well, he could damn well do better than that.

Which was probably what he intended in the first place. Umber was a sneaky bastard, sometimes, but it was one of the things Nick liked about him so much. One of the things that made him so damn appealing to surrender to.

He turned off the lights and pulled down the shutters, then let himself out. The late autumn light was dimming already, the sky a kind of velvety gray with the first touches of sunset pinking its edges. He smelled something like snow behind the scents of the city, the coming of winter. He'd never seen Westerley in the snow before. He was looking forward to it.

He smiled. To think that a few months ago he would have done anything to leave the place.

The bell over the door tinkled, followed by the rhythm of heels on the wooden floor. Nick grinned. It had to be some kind of unwritten law of retail that a customer always came in right when the shop was about to close.

"Excuse me, you wouldn't happen to be Jacob Umber, would you?"

"No, sorry." Nick looked up and automatically said, "How can I help you?" as he looked the customer up and down. A woman, maybe in her mid-thirties, conservatively dressed, with a blonde pixie cut. She looked like a suburban mom dressed for business, complete with the glint of her thin-framed glasses.

"He is the business owner?"

"Ye-es, this is his store." Nick frowned. "Do you have a message for him?"

"I'd like to speak to Mr. Umber, if he has the time." She took out a business card and laid it facedown on the counter. "My number is on my card.

"And your name is?"

"Special Agent Siobhan Marks."

Nick kept his face impassive. "Special agent with the...?"

"With the Federal Bureau of Investigation."

He picked up the card and flipped it over. Well, either she was telling the truth, or she had some very good fake FBI business cards printed. "What shall I tell him it's regarding?"

"I'd like to ask him some questions regarding the previous owner of this store, Margaret Mason."

"Sure." He tucked the card in his front shirt pocket. "I'll let him know when I see him, Agent Marks."

She looked around the shop with a kind of affectedly casual interest. "Have you been working here long, Mr..."

"Nick," he said, holding out his hand. "Nick Kurosawa."

She shook it with a firm, steady grip, but her smile did not quite reach her very blue eyes. "Nice to meet you, Nick."

"Likewise, uh, Siobhan." He grinned. "I assume it's all right to call you that?"

"Sure." Her smile widened to match his.

"And no, I haven't been working here long." He ran a hand through his hair. "Technically, I don't really work here at all—I'm Mr. Umber's PA."

"Do you mean you're his secretary?"

"Sure, sometimes." He laughed at her quizzical look. "No, I'm a personal assistant in a broader sense. Mr. Umber is disabled, and I was hired to help him out."

"Oh!"

It seemed to take her aback. Nick was suddenly uncomfortable—she hadn't known, and he felt he'd somehow overstepped a boundary by telling her in such a casual way. Why hadn't he just said he worked at the store? He wanted to kick himself.

"Well," she said, filling the uncomfortable silence, "please do pass on my message to Mr. Umber. Do you know if he has a person number, actually? There doesn't seem to be any listed for him."

He shook his head. "Mr. Umber is kind of old-fashioned that way. The store has a number, but he doesn't have a cell phone or anything."

"No home telephone?"

Nick thought a moment. "Now that you mention it, I've never seen one."

She grinned. The crookedness of it was oddly charming, breaking the suburban-mom mask of her face into something younger and more mischievous. "I suppose I've done the modern equivalent of leaving my calling card. Hopefully that'll satisfy someone as old-fashioned as Mr. Umber."

He laughed, the tension that had coiled in his chest easing a little. "I'm sure it'll charm him, put like that."

"I'm glad to hear it." She made an odd little gesture, as if she were tipping an invisible hat to him. "Nice to meet you, again, and you have a good day, all right?

"You too." He watched her leave, shaking his head a little. *Wonder what she wants.*

Half a minute later, just long enough that she wouldn't still be outside and think he'd rushed to do it after she left, he locked up the shop. The closer he got to being able to leave, the happier he felt, but not because the day was done. He was happy because he'd be going home to Mr. Umber.

Going home. That was a treacherous thing to think, he knew as much, but he couldn't stop the warm glow coursing through him at the thought.

*

The grocery store that Umber had directed him to was fancier than he'd usually shop in, even if he'd had the money at hand. Umber's black card would buy him anything he desired, of course, but the power of it unnerved him. His family had never been anywhere near rich. Even the janitors in a grocery store like this could probably smell that he didn't belong there, that he wouldn't know what wine to pair with what cheese.

It isn't my power though. It's his.

Somehow, this thought calmed him almost immediately. He wasn't here for himself—he was here as Umber's man. All he had to do was think of what Mr. Umber would want, what would please him, and he knew that he wouldn't err.

Nick picked out the ingredients for a simple risotto. When he was done, he walked all the way from the store to Umber's apartment rather than taking the bus, even though it took him half an hour longer. He couldn't say why he wanted to, except that it deferred the pleasure of coming home, and deferring pleasure was a pleasure in itself.

When he arrived at Clarebrook Towers, the sun was low enough to paint the glass-and-copper cladding the reddish-gold of autumn leaves and blood. He looked up, finding Umber's apartment with his eyes, the penthouse windows lit up by the sunset. The shades would be drawn, he knew, except for in the living room, where there'd be a shaft of light falling across the Turkish rug.

He nodded to the security guard and slid his key card into the slot of the penthouse elevator. His heart was beating a steady, even rhythm, but it seemed to fill his chest nonetheless, as if it had grown to five times its usual size.

When he walked into the apartment, the first thing he heard was the soft hum of Nina Simone over the sound system, which followed him from room to room. Umber wasn't in the living room, or in the kitchen. Nick unpacked his shopping, singing along under his breath.

"Now I've got a guy loves to stay home at night," he sang. "He really knows how to treat me right." He started chopping onions, fennel, and garlic, tossed them in a pan with a knob of butter, and poured a glass of wine.

"I didn't know you were a Nina Simone fan."

He turned away from his cooking. Umber was leaning over the kitchen island, head tilted as he watched Nick at work. "My mom used to listen to her a lot when I was a kid. Guess I picked up an appreciation." He turned down the heat and picked up the crystal wine glass, handing it over to him.

"Thank you, Nick." He took a sip. "This is very nice."

"Glad you think so, Mr. Umber." He smiled and turned back to the risotto, tossing half his tumbler of wine in with the rice. Umber didn't say anything else, just took a seat at the kitchen aisle and watched him cook. Nina Simone changed to a soft jazz instrumental that Nick didn't recognize.

"I'm assuming all went well at the store today?"

"Quiet as usual," Nick said, then remembered Agent Marks's card in his pocket. "One kind of unusual visitor though."

"Oh?"

He took out the card and slid it across the kitchen island. "An FBI agent stopped by and said she'd like to speak to you about the lady who used to own your shop. Margaret Mason?"

"Did she?" If Umber was at all surprised, he didn't show it. He tucked the card away. "I suppose I'll get back to her."

Well, that's dealt with. Nick put it out of his mind and turned back to the stove. "I hope you like risotto."

"In fact, I love it."

He was glad he was facing the stove and that Umber couldn't see his shit-eating grin. "It will be done in five minutes. Then it just needs to sit."

"Very good. Please also bring me my wine from the kitchen. I'd like to watch television while I eat tonight, so please bring a tray to the living room."

"Yes, Mr. Umber." He bowed his head, ever so slightly. "I'll be right there."

Umber put his half-full wineglass on the island counter and left the kitchen. A tray, he had said, not trays. That meant one tray for both of them? He took one from the cupboard, a delicately filigreed oval of silver. He served up two bowls, placed Umber's half-full wineglass from the counter on the tray alongside them, and carried them into the living room.

Umber was already seated, the television playing what looked to Nick like a nature documentary. He knelt in front of the sofa and proffered the tray.

Umber clucked his tongue. "A nice sight, but not very practical. Put your bowl and my glass of wine on the coffee table and hand me the tray, please."

Nick did, and looked up at Umber, waiting.

He raised his eyebrows fractionally. "Please eat, Nick, I would hate to see this go to waste."

All right, I'm supposed to...eat on the floor, I guess. He licked his lips and turned away from Umber, toward the television, and picked up his bowl off the coffee table. At least risotto was relatively easy to eat without putting the bowl on a table. He'd tasted it all through cooking, but not since it had sat and rested, letting the cheese melt through it. He took a spoonful and smiled. It was good, if he didn't say so himself.

They finished eating. He washed the dishes, dried them, and put them away, then poured another glass of wine and took it back into the living room. Umber had turned off the television and put on some music, soft drums and sweet clarinet. He took the glass of wine from Nick with a smile.

It was so ordinary, in a way. Nick wasn't doing anything that ten thousand devoted boyfriends weren't doing at that very moment, without any thought they were giving service to anyone. Cooking, dishes, pouring a glass of wine... It wasn't the actions, but the intent behind them. He was serving Umber's pleasure, being useful to him, just as much as he was when he drove him to a meeting with a client or bent over to take a spanking.

The spankings might actually be more for my benefit. He grinned at the thought.

"Nick," Umber said, and their eyes met. He tilted his head, smiling a little. "Would you kneel for me?"

Ah. *There* was something ten thousand boyfriends weren't quite doing that very second. He melted to his knees. Umber tangled his fingers in Nick's hair and pulled him closer until he was leaning up against the sofa—and Umber's knee.

He made a small satisfied noise. Nick allowed himself to close his eyes, resting his head and luxuriating in the feeling of Umber threading his fingers through his hair.

"Nick."

"Mmm?"

"I would like you to stay here tonight. That is not an order," he said quickly. "It is simply a preference."

"I would like it too," Nick murmured, not opening his eyes.

"You would?"

As if you need to ask. He looked up at Umber, taking his hand from the top of his head and moving it down so he was cupping Nick's cheek. Nick's own hand rested on top of Umber's, stroking the back of it with his thumb. "I would," he said with a low, even voice.

Umber parted his lips as if he were about to speak, then closed his mouth again. Kiss me, Nick wanted to say, but the words died in his throat. Umber pulled his hand away, very gently, but stopped to stroke his thumb over the edge of Nick's jaw. "I should warn you," he said, sounding very solemn, "that I have been known to snore."

*

Nick couldn't stop the laugh that welled out of him, and Umber grinned back—a true, impish grin that made him look twenty years younger. "I used to bunk with twenty overgrown teenagers, back when I was in boot camp," Nick said. "I can survive a little snore."

"If you say so," Umber said, the grin fading a little. He stood up slowly. "Please run me a bath, Nick? Once it's run, you should use the guest bathroom to shower."

A hitch of nervous desire spiked upward from the base of Nick's spine into his stomach. "Should I get dressed again, afterward?"

Umber shook his head. "There are some pajama trousers in the guest bedroom drawers. Please wear those. No shirt."

He nodded. "Yes, Mr. Umber."

Umber caressed his neck with two fingers, resting them on Nick's jugular, as if he were a doctor taking his pulse. "Now, please, Nick."

He didn't need to say it twice. Nick rose to his feet and went to the bathroom, starting the now-familiar ritual of preparing Umber's bath: testing the temperature of the water, pouring in the Epsom salts, adding the soap, sometimes a drop or two of essential oils. Lavender if he knew Umber had been restless, or eucalyptus if his muscles had seemed sore.

When the bath was full, he turned off the tap and went back into the living room. Umber was unbuttoning his shirt already, and the breath caught in Nick's throat. He still hadn't seen him naked—somehow that denial had managed to heighten his appreciation for every inch of skin he could see. The bare triangle at his opened collar drew Nick's eyes as if it were a magnet.

"Your bath is ready," he said, his throat thick with desire.

"Thank you, Nick." Umber's eyes sparkled. "Go and shower, and wait in the guest bedroom when you are done."

"Of course," he said, and went.

By the time he'd stripped off and stepped in the shower, he was painfully hard. He wondered if Umber had known this would happen—scratch that, of course he knew it would. Nick's cock was almost flat against his stomach as he washed. He had to be careful not to brush up against it, or he might have come near spontaneously.

How many weeks had it been now? Too many—and Umber had barely touched him, beyond teasing grazes. He'd certainly not demanded the sexual service Nick had happily volunteered. Would happily volunteer, anytime Umber asked.

He toweled himself off, trying to will his embarrassing excitement to subside at least a little. He had a feeling the pajama pants Umber had mentioned wouldn't leave much to the imagination.

When he was dry, he took them out of the drawers and looked at them with baleful eyes. They were silk, finespun, the color of a cloud on a rainy day. Beautifully made, and yes, they would outline every inch of him in fine detail.

Well. Umber had given him instructions. He wasn't about to disobey them.

Nick pulled on the pajama pants, leaving off his underwear. Somehow, he felt even more exposed than if he were naked. His cock had softened a little, but was still obscenely visible through the thin silk. He shuddered a little and stood at the foot of the guest bed, waiting.

When Umber opened the door, Nick had gone into a kind of fugue state—half blank, half aroused, on the bare edge of being awake. He shifted back into an attentive pose, and then realized he didn't know what to do with his arms, so put them behind his back in a loose approximation of standing at ease.

Umber wore his white terry cloth robe. His hair was combed back from his forehead, and his expression was solemn. If his earlier grin had dropped twenty years off of him, this added about ten. He looked severe and stern, and terribly handsome.

He glanced down between Nick's legs. His cock was stirring again, hardening more with every moment. He could feel Umber's eyes on him, his gaze palpable as fingertips. "You're excited," he said softly. It was stating the obvious, but somehow it made Nick's mouth go dry. "Just from waiting for me?"

"Yes."

"Mm." Umber's hand cupped the silk-clad outline of his cock. Nick thought he might come right there and then. Somewhere, distantly, he realized it was the first time Umber had touched his cock. "I can't say that I'm not flattered."

"Please," he said, hating the whimpering tone to his voice.

"What are you asking for, Nick?" Umber rested his hand there, not moving it, not stroking him, just holding his cock.

"I—I don't know."

"If you don't know, then perhaps it will behoove you to sleep like this," Umber said, meditatively, still holding onto his cock. "Perhaps I want you to fall asleep still hard for me."

Nick breathed in sharply but said nothing else. There were no words that came to him.

"Unless, of course, you have something else in mind? Something you want to ask of me?"

Please, please, please—it echoed through him like the tolling of a bell. He wanted Umber to never let go of him. He wanted him to jerk him roughly through the silk. He wanted him to smack his cock sharply and reprimand him for allowing such a display. He wanted Umber, hot and tight around him, riding him, using him as a prop for his own pleasure, coming apart on top of him. He couldn't ask it, any of it, and Umber knew it—was trying to squeeze the words out, almost literally.

"Tell me." His voice low, he pressed himself against Nick, so the thrum of it rumbled through Nick's chest. Nick's cock twitched under Umber's hand. "And don't," he said sharply, "even think about coming until you do."

"P-please," Nick managed at last, "I want..."

"Tell me."

The words seemed to be made of paper-mache, thickening his tongue, stopping up his mouth. He was supposed to be...what? Made of stone, a robot, wanting nothing, here only to serve. The perfect blank slate. But that wasn't what Umber wanted. No, he was more demanding than that. He wanted Nick, in all his dumb imperfection. Nick couldn't really understand why.

"I want," he said, "you. To feel you. To come because of you."

"Good," Umber said, stroking him gently through the silk. "Very good, Nick. You have done so well."

"Ah!" It was too much. "I—I can't hold on—"

Umber squeezed his cock tightly. "Then come for me."

That was all it took for Nick to thoroughly ruin Umber's silk pajama pants. He spent himself with such force it left him weak-kneed and gasping, and the entire time, Umber did not let go of him—warm and insistent, his hand in a vise-like grip around his sensitive cock.

Umber smiled a little. "Perhaps I should have done this before you showered. Go clean yourself up, Nick; there's another pair of trousers in the drawer." He hesitated a moment. "Then please join me in my bedroom, if you'd be so kind."

Umber left him then—to go wash his hands, probably, and Nick bent double to stop himself from laughing. It was half-hysterical, that laughter. He felt knocked off-balance, in more ways than one.

This wasn't sex as he knew it. It wasn't even domination as he knew it. Most of the men he knew would have fucked him, or have him fuck them, by now. Most of them would have demanded his mouth, his ass, would have whipped him or gagged him.

What had Umber done tonight, really? Had him make dinner. Had him kneel so he could stroke his hair. It was so...gentle. And yet, it had shaken him up in a way that no hot and heavy session of leather-sex had managed.

Is it because of how I feel about him? It was frightening to contemplate.

He stripped off the soaked pajama trousers and rinsed himself quickly, roughly drying himself with the same towel he'd used after his shower. Then he slipped into another pair of trousers—*how did he get these in my size, anyway?*— and padded down the hallway to Umber's bedroom.

Umber had shed the terry cloth robe and was wearing pajamas—proper, old-fashioned pajamas in a touchingly tacky tartan pattern. He sat on the edge of his bed, eying Nick with a hint of reproach. "You took your time."

Nick bowed his head. "I'm sorry, Mr. Umber. I was distracted."

"Hm. I suppose I can understand that." He looked at Nick—no, through him, really, into some distant place Nick couldn't see. "Nick, would you like to sleep in my bedroom?"

Umber was always precise with his language; he'd said bedroom, not bed. Nick lowered his gaze. "Where would you like me to sleep?"

"On the floor," Umber said. "Beside me."

Nick made a soft sound. He couldn't tell if he was disappointed, or if this was exactly what he wanted. "Of course, Mr. Umber," he said, almost in a whisper.

"There is a futon under my bed. Pull it out."

He did. Umber reached over and grabbed one of his pillows, handing it down to Nick with a soft smile. Nick took it; it was still warm with the ghost of Umber's skin. "Thank you," he said, and now it was a whisper.

Umber ran a hand through Nick's hair, then retreated to his nest of blankets and turned over. "Sleep well, Nick," he said, his voice slightly muffled.

"Good night, Mr. Umber."

Nick lay on his back, hand on his chest. It wasn't cold, but it was strange to lie there without a blanket. He stared at the ceiling in the dark until he saw patterns form and shift. Only when Umber began to snore, as promised, did he slip into a deep and dreamless sleep.

*

Nick woke in the small hours of the night. For a moment, he didn't realize where he was—why there wasn't a blanket on him, why the mattress below him felt different. Then the slow knowledge of exactly where he was washed over him like warm water, and something bright and hard twisted into a not-unpleasant knot in his stomach.

I'm with Umber. Where he put me.

Umber's breathing was steady with sleep. Nick wanted to sit up and watch him, but instead, he stayed on the futon, one hand on his chest, feeling his slow and steady heartbeat. This wasn't normal, some voice told him—it wasn't normal, to sleep like a dog on the floor beside someone and feel like you belonged there. But whatever weak protest, whatever appeal to normality the voice could come up with, it was outvoted by the steady, peaceful thrum of Nick's heart. By his nightmare-less sleep.

He fell asleep again with startling ease, and when he woke up once more, it was to someone softly calling his name.

"Nick? Are you all right?"

"Yes." He spoke before he was even fully awake. "Yes, Mr. Umber, I'm here. I'm all right."

He sat up, blinking a little. Sunlight was half-visible from the hallway, the east-facing windows catching the morning light. Umber was half propped on his elbow, blinking owlishly at Nick. He looked…for some reason the word that came to Nick's mind was "adorable."

He suppressed a laugh; it wasn't exactly the word that usually came to mind when a man ordered you to sleep on the floor beside him. Not that Nick had much experience with that. He was extrapolating from the other things he'd had done to him before. Which, to be fair, weren't much like what Umber did to—with—him, at all.

"It's Sunday," Umber said.

Nick grinned. "Do you want breakfast in bed?"

"It's your day off," he reminded him.

He shrugged. "Good. Means I can choose what I want to do with my time."

There was a moment of silence. The texture of it was somehow off—thicker, colder than their usual companionable quiet. *Is he regretting allowing me to sleep here, after all?*

He got up and wordlessly stripped the futon before sliding it back under Umber's bed, then put the used linen down the laundry chute. Umber watched him from the bed, unmoving. The hairs on the back of Nick's neck prickled with his regard. He set his jaw. He wasn't about to let Umber just dismiss him, like…

Like an employee? *Come on, Kurosawa.*

"Is there anything you need, Mr. Umber?"

"No," he said. "I'll be quite fine, thank you, N—Mr. Kurosawa."

Nick inclined his head with a little smile. "Then I'll see you on Monday."

When he walked out of Clarebrook Towers, the winter air hit him like a blast chiller. He shivered and jammed his hands in his pockets, looking up at the pale blue sky.

He sighed. Suddenly, he badly wanted someone to talk to—someone who'd actually talk. His first instinct was to call Alex, but when he took his phone out, something made him hesitate. He scrolled down his not-very-robust list of contacts until he found Gordon's number, and hit dial.

*

A few hours later, they were in Nick's favorite coffee shop together, warming their hands over king-sized lattes. Gordon was smiling at him, a little quizzically. Nick had asked if he'd like to come out for a coffee "just as friends." Nick knew friends was stretching it, between them—Gordon must have thought the same.

"Heard you showed up at the play party," Gordon said after a few minutes' worth of vague small talk. "Didn't end up staying long."

"I guess it wasn't my scene, after all. But...thanks." Nick tried for a smile. "Really."

"Well, you're welcome back, if you ever change your mind." Gordon looked at him with an uncomfortably penetrating stare. "Not that I think you will."

"Yeah. I guess not."

There was a moment of silence. Nick took a sip of his coffee.

"So." Gordon grinned. "You said you wanted to talk. So talk."

Nick sighed. "All right, well, I...I met someone." He wrapped his hand around the mug, unable to stop himself from smiling a little. "Someone who's into the same kind of kink I am."

"Someone who won't jam a puppy tail in you without checking with you first, you mean," Gordon deadpanned, and Nick laughed.

"Yeah, pretty much."

Gordon rubbed his forehead. "Yeah, I'm still embarrassed about that. But, sorry, go on."

"We've been—together? Doing stuff together, I guess, for a few weeks now. It's…" He breathed out as heat crept up his face. "I've never felt like this before, ever. I thought that what I wanted, that I couldn't find it, that it was, I dunno. I'm not into rubber or leather, I'm kind of a private guy, but I'm not vanilla and never will be. This guy understands that. Wants the same things."

Gordon raised his eyebrows. "But…?"

"But what?"

"Just that I can sense a 'but' coming. Or else you've just invited me here to brag about it, which I don't think is your style."

"We don't fuck," Nick said, spitting it out bluntly. "We don't even kiss. It's like he barely wants to touch me. I just serve him; I don't…do anything for him sexually."

"And you'd like it to."

He grimaced. "I guess I'm that obvious, huh?"

Gordon smiled and nodded. "You've got it bad. I can tell that much. You know what you need to do, right?"

"What's that?"

Gordon laughed. "Seriously? Talk to him. You've obviously managed to negotiate something pretty hot between you, so why not just say you'd like to take it in a different direction?"

Nick blinked. "I…guess that's an option."

"Of course it's an option. C'mon, Nick, you're both adults. You didn't have any problem telling me what you wanted."

Nick grinned and shook his head. "That's the thing. It's easy to tell people what I don't want. When it comes to what I do want…"

"Ah." Understanding, and something like sympathy, dawned on Gordon's face. "Yeah. That can be an issue."

"Not for you, I bet."

"Heh. Not usually, not when it comes to..." He made a vague hand gesture. "Not when it comes to telling cute boys what I'd like them to do for me, no. But when it comes to something a little closer to the heart, well..."

Nick nodded. "It's not so easy then, huh?"

"Not so easy," Gordon agreed. "But look, unless there's something wrong with this guy, I know he's hot for you. Just come out and say it."

"I dunno, doesn't need to be something wrong with him for him not to want that. He could be asexual, or, I dunno. Maybe he keeps his kink separate from his love life. Maybe he wants someone vanilla to take to restaurants and the opera while he's got a boy to beat at home."

"Sure," Gordon agreed. "But you don't think so, do you?"

Nick cocked his head and looked at Gordon. "Why's that?"

"You don't seem to be the type of guy who'd go for being someone's side piece, and you seem to have had some hot times. Maybe he is ace, I don't know, but that doesn't mean you can't negotiate for what you need either."

Nick looked away and bit his lip. "What if he can't give it to me?"

"Then I guess you've got a choice to make."

"Yeah." He sighed. "I know you're right. It's just..."

"It's just taking that step out into the dark, huh?"

"That's poetic of you."

"That's right," Gordon said, getting up and clapping him on the shoulder, "I'm a poet. You want another coffee?"

Nick shook his head. "Thanks, Gordon. Not just for the coffee."

He nodded. "It's all right, kid. And—hey, good luck."

*

Talk to him: Gordon's advice had been deceptively simple, and like all deceptively simple things was harder than Nick had imagined.

When Nick was on the clock, there was an unspoken agreement that he and Umber didn't talk about...their thing. Once the day was done, well. There never seemed to be a right time, or else the words would dry up on Nick's tongue the moment he'd formulated them.

That, and I'm scared. He could admit that much to himself. There was always the chance that if he said, "Hey, I'd like something more," he'd end up with less, or nothing at all. Maybe he could square himself with being allowed to kneel for Umber, to sleep by his side when he allowed it, to get rewarded with an occasional (much too occasional) spanking, and accept that the rest of what he wanted just...wasn't going to happen for them.

His dreams told him differently. They started to get— loud, strange, full of distorted versions of himself and Umber.

He woke up panting to the dream-image of Umber straddling him, snarling at him with vicious anger, threatening to kick the shit out of him in a very un-Umberish way. The dream had left him both unsettled and horribly turned on. Nick knew something had to give—he had to say something.

He was going to say something first thing in the morning, working hours be damned, but he didn't. He was going to say something over their shared lunch, but he didn't. Then it was going to be in the taxi, but something stopped him, and then finally, he found himself standing in front of Umber's door and suddenly, irrevocably frozen on the mat.

Umber, half a footstep in front of him, turned around with a quizzical look. "Are you all right?"

Nick swallowed. Opened his mouth. Swallowed again. *Say something, goddamn it!*

"Mr. Kurosawa?"

"I—look—Mr. Umber..."

"What is it, Nick?"

"Do you actually want me?"

The words were out of his mouth before he'd had a chance to think them through, and he winced. It wasn't what he'd meant to say. He sounded whiny, petulant. It wasn't at all the relaxed, adult conversation he'd wanted to have.

Umber seemed to sense as much, and waited a long moment before responding. "Perhaps we should have this conversation inside the apartment?"

There was nobody in the hallway—there would be nobody in the hallway if Mr. Umber didn't let them up—but Nick could see his point nonetheless. He stepped inside, cheeks burning, and closed the door behind him.

"What do you mean by 'actually wanting you'?"

Nick breathed out huffily. "You know what I mean. Just...wanting me. Wanting this."

"Of course I do," Umber said in a slightly baffled tone. "Why else would I be doing it?"

"It's just—" Nick swallowed. "I guess I worry that you're kind of. I don't know. Humoring me."

"Humoring you."

Nick had to close his eyes, his fists clenched at his sides. He made himself count to ten, as if he were angry. When he spoke, his words fell out in a rush, stumbling-tongued and rough-voiced. "You don't fuck me," he said, finding refuge in the bluntness. "Or tie me up, or even spank me that much, and. I don't know. You get something out of it, but maybe I want more."

"Oh, Nick."

The tenderness in Umber's voice almost undid him, but the thrill of something darker in it was like a slap: both bracing and terribly arousing all at once. Nick wanted, very badly, to kneel for him, but he stayed upright and forced himself to open his eyes.

"Mr. Umber." He swallowed; it was a narrow thing that he had not called him sir. Some reckless bravery in him made him add something else that he'd never called him before. "Jacob."

Umber sucked in a breath. "On your knees. Go to the sofa."

Nick went to his knees so fast they cracked against the floor. He didn't care—didn't even feel it. On his hands and knees, he crawled toward the sofa, Umber following close behind him. He could feel the warmth of him beside him.

"Take off your shirt."

With trembling fingers, Nick unbuttoned his shirt and took it off. Still kneeling, he folded it as carefully as he could. It wasn't quite military precision, not with his hands shaking the way they were, but it was an effort toward it, at least. He handed it to Umber, who took it without comment and laid it on a nearby shelf and then sat down on the sofa. Nick remained on his knees, looking up at him. Waiting.

"Take off my shoes."

Halfway through undoing Umber's laces, Nick's hands stopped shaking. He'd snapped into that thoughtless presence, that strange grace he sometimes had when Umber commanded him. He undid both shoes, slipped them off Umber's feet, and put them aside. Then he waited. If it'd been another man, another time, he'd have moved to undo Umber's zipper, started working his trousers down his legs—why else would a man command you to kneel and start undressing him?—but he didn't. Umber would tell him what he needed to do. All he had to do was act when it was required.

"Hands and knees again, if you please."

He obeyed. A moment later, the weight of Umber's feet settled on the small of his back. He sagged a little under their weight, and then straightened his back.

Umber gave a soft, satisfied sigh. "There. That's very nice."

Nick swallowed and closed his eyes. A warmth suffused him from top to bottom, sweet and all-encompassing, transmuting the restless heat that had throbbed through him in a strange kind of alchemy. It was that same sunlit feeling he had when Umber smiled at him, when he proved his worth to him, except stronger, bigger. Magnified, as if his heart were under a telescope.

"Move a little closer, Nick."

He did. Umber swung his legs over Nick's back as if he were an ottoman, and Nick was rewarded with Umber's hand playing softly at his hair, stroking his cheek. Between the weight of his legs on his back and the softness of his touch, Nick was in heaven. His thoughts were wordless, but they all amounted to the same thing: This was where he belonged. This was his place. This was his purpose.

When Umber took his legs off of Nick's back, he breathed out with physical relief and bone-deep disappointment. He knew then that Umber had noticed the slight tremors in his muscles. *If I were in better shape, if I'd kept up my training, I could have held still longer…*

Before he could get any deeper into his self-recrimination, Umber leaned over him and tilted his head up so he could look into Nick's eyes. Umber's eyes were nearly black, the pupils blown wide, the remnants of the gray-green iris dark in the living room's muted lights. "You've pleased me, very much," he said. Leaving no room for Nick's self-doubt. "Let me show you how very much I want you."

Then he did something Nick was not expecting, and kissed him.

It was almost chaste, almost hesitant. Barely more than a touch—an experimental press of mouth to mouth. When Umber dared to part his lips, Nick gasped. All that heat that had suffused itself into warm happiness returned, twice as hard, bowling Nick over with a desire so deeply physical it made his head spin. *Fuck, he's barely even kissing me, how does he do this to me?*

Umber drew away from him, leaning back onto the sofa. His breaths were deep and even. "That's enough of that for now," he said, and Nick could have almost laughed at the schoolmaster tone in his voice. Almost, because beneath the prissy coolness of his words desire thrummed like something dark and massive moving beneath thin ice.

*

After a moment he rose from the sofa. Nick remained on his knees, waiting. "Look at me," he said.

Nick looked up. Umber took his chin in his hand, steadying him. The other hand played over his cheekbones, the curve of his jawline. When the first slap came it was almost a caress, barely anything that could be called a slap. It certainly didn't hurt, but Nick gasped out loud nonetheless. Umber held his face steady while he built up a jagged rhythm of slaps, soft as suede dragged on skin. Too soft—Nick wanted to beg for him to hit him harder, to hurt him, but he kept his mouth shut, silent except for his ragged breathing.

He stopped for a moment, but didn't release Nick's face. He turned it from side to side, as if studying it. "This frustrates you, doesn't it?"

Nick made an incoherent noise. Finally, he managed a guttural "yes."

"Why?"

Nick swallowed. *God, he likes asking his questions, doesn't he?* It was a bitter voice, from some cold place inside him. *Likes it better than playing with you.*

Umber slapped him in earnest then, hard—hard enough that his head would have whipped from side to side if he hadn't been holding it steady. The imprint of his slap burned on Nick's cheek. The bitter voice had gone silent—every single thought had gone silent.

"Why?" Umber asked again, merciless.

"Because," Nick said slowly, speaking as if his mouth were full of cotton wool, "you weren't doing *that.*"

"Why don't you ask for it, Nick? Has nobody ever told you it's polite to ask for what you want?" He shook Nick's head, just a little, the way you might shake a dog that had misbehaved.

Nick realized Umber wasn't just talking about now, here—he was talking about everything Nick had left unspoken, the desires he'd kept stoppered up until they'd almost curdled inside him. "I want it to please you." The words ground in his throat. Umber had forced them out of him. Hot shame colored his cheeks, and wished he could take them back.

"Oh, Nick." Umber's face was unreadable up until the moment he smiled. It wasn't a friendly smile—it was cold and sharp and perfect. "But it does please me."

He hit him again, with precise force, and again, and again, until Nick was gasping, until the blush in his cheeks had turned to stinging fire. It burned through him, reaching at last the cold place inside of him where those cynical whispers came from. Umber liked this, Umber wanted this, but he'd been holding back, and finally allowed himself the license.

He stopped at last, breathing hard. "I'm not done with you. I'm going to mark you, Nick, I'm going to leave bruises on you that will last for days, and you will know each and every one of them for my work."

Please, yes, he wanted to gasp, but no words came.

"Get up and get your pants and underpants off. Over the sofa."

Nick moved as if he were a machine and Umber had just punched in the right code. He stripped down with the kind of speed he'd only had when he and thirty other guys were in line for the same shower, and threw himself over the sofa. For a moment, he wondered whether Umber would use his belt, or his hand, or some other implement, but then he realized it didn't matter—that any of it, all of it, was welcome. Was craved.

He couldn't stop himself from shaking a little. He was naked, vulnerable, while Umber stalked around him still in his fine suit. Never mind the fact that Nick was half a head taller, and outweighed him. Never mind the fact that Nick was a trained (if slightly out of shape) soldier and Umber a disabled man almost two decades his senior. At the moment, Umber had him completely in his power.

The first blow came on the curve of his ass: Umber's hand, laying into him with startling force. He grunted and thrust his hips forward, half instinctively trying to dodge the blow, half grinding into the side of the sofa as if he were a dog in heat, desperate for any friction.

"This," Umber said, "is to warm you up."

Then he continued, spanking Nick with a humiliating efficiency. Images flashed through Nick's mind, old fantasies of stern schoolmasters, of cruel drill instructors, of muscled men in dingy bars that dragged him home and used him with rough hands. They all seemed pale and anemic, compared to this, the simplicity of being bent over and spanked.

When he stopped, Nick almost begged for him to go on, until he remembered what Umber had said when it began.

This is to warm you up.

Umber left him for a moment. When he returned, he pressed something hard against Nick's skin. He froze, knowing instantly what it was. When had Umber gotten a cane?

The cane whistled through the air. The sting of contact burned, a line of white fire against his skin—and that was just the first strike. Umber had promised to mark him, and Nick knew he was. A cane used with such force would leave stripes on him that would last for days. Maybe weeks.

And all I want to do is thank him. Oh, God.

Then the cane whistled again and struck his thighs, and Nick screamed.

"Yes," Umber said, "yes, that's good. Let me hear you. It's fine, Nick. You can be as loud as you want."

It broke something in him, some chain he hadn't even known was there, some last bastion of reserve. Any thoughts were burned out of him as Umber alternated between cane, and hand, and belt, painting his skin, making him a masterpiece of bruises. Every stroke, every hit, said mine, mine, mine, and Nick surrendered to it wholly.

After a timeless span, it slowed—then ended. Nick was crying, half in joy and half in agony, the sound of it like a wild thing baying at the moon. Then Umber's hand on his bruised back, cool and gentle, brought him back from that howling edge, back from the thoughtless and wordless place where he'd found himself and into his own body again. "If I strike you a few more times," Umber said, low-voiced, "I will draw blood."

Nick whimpered and ground his hips against the sofa. The leather was wet with his sweat and his precome. He didn't know whether to beg for Umber to continue, to finally make him bleed, or to beg for him to stop.

"Nick." Umber stroked his hair, very gently. "Nick, you were so good. So very good for me."

No, please, Nick wanted to say—it was too much, Umber's effusive praise hurt as much as the stroke of a cane, and left deeper marks.

"I know you would take it from me, if I made you bleed," he murmured. "I know you would allow me to do that, and thank me for it. And it is a gift beyond measure, Nick, that kind of—that kind of trust."

He managed another whimper. He was shaking, the endorphin rush from his beating fraying at the edges.

"But I need something else from you now, Nick. I need you to stand up, and look at me, and tell me how you are feeling."

Somehow, it had seemed impossible until Umber had spoken the words. He breathed in and out slowly a few times, gathering himself. Then he stood up, only a little shakily. As he moved, he could feel every inch of where Umber had marked him. He knew he would be sore for a long time, and the knowledge made him feel almost smug. "I'm all right," he said, his voice ragged but clear. "Yeah. I'm—I'm all right."

Umber took his chin in his hand and looked at him with narrowed eyes, as if searching him for any possible dissembling. "I would like you to take a hot bath. Prepare it the way you would for me."

Nick made an involuntary sound, low and pathetic, and Umber blinked at him.

"Would you prefer a shower, Nick?"

"No." His tongue felt thick. "I just...I just don't want to be alone."

"Ah." Umber smiled up at him, then took his hand and pulled him over to the love seat. It was barely big enough to fit both of them, but if Nick curled up and laid his head on Umber's lap...

Then it fit them just fine.

"Nick, there's a blanket in the ottoman."

Nick pulled it over clumsily and opened it, grabbed a tartan blanket, and handed it over to Umber. He wrapped it around Nick's shoulders, covering him from shoulder to knee, leaving his feet bare and a little cold. He didn't mind though. He was warm enough—he was where he should be. "I should be doing this for you," he muttered.

"I don't think so, Nick," Umber said fondly. "It is my turn to take care of you, now."

Somehow, he didn't feel like arguing with that.

*

He woke up slowly, too aware of being both exquisitely comfortable and in a fair amount of pain. Comfortable, because he was in Umber's guest bed; in pain, because his back, thighs, shoulders and ass were lined with what felt like a hundred crisscrossing bruises. He shifted slightly, his tender skin sliding against Umber's Egyptian cotton bedsheets. Their luxuriance felt odd. The last time he'd been this bruised was after he'd taken a hard landing jumping out of a helicopter during a training exercise with local forces in Uganda. He'd gone to sleep that night on a cot, wrapped in a scratchy blanket. His life back then might have been improved by 300-thread-count sheets.

He sat up in bed, blinking against the light. Faint stipples of blood were vivid against the white sheets—some of the harshest strikes from the cane had bled, just a little, in the night. For half a second, he was worried Umber would be upset at the ruined sheets...but then he remembered him washing Nick's tender skin with a soft, warm cloth, then leading Nick to the bedroom by the hand, sitting beside him and stroking his forehead until he fell asleep. A man who did that, a man like Umber, was not going to complain about a few pinpricks of blood on his white sheets.

Had he really been there, until Nick fell asleep? Surely it couldn't just have been Nick's imagination that had summoned that up. No, the sense memory was too real, no matter how strangely...ideal it seemed. He could still feel Umber's cool, callused fingers stroking him. Making sure he was safe, that he was all right.

A bolt of shame went through him—God, how fucking tired must Umber have been? The caning he'd given Nick would have tired out any man, and Nick hadn't even prepared his customary bath to soothe his aches before sleep. He must be feeling like shit right now.

He got out of bed. After stretching his sore muscles, he realized his bruises didn't hurt as much as he'd anticipated. They were sore, present on his skin, but from the way he'd surrendered to Umber's blows, he expected to be black and blue.

He looked over his shoulder, twisting to get a better look at his backside. There were a few heavy stripes there, yes, laid with precision. The one that had bled a little was on his thighs, and looked the darkest of them all. His ass had the overall pinkness he sometimes got after a thorough spanking, but overall, there was nothing that hurt worse than he might have gotten after a day hiking, give or take a few falls.

The cane-strikes, though...they would linger long, their soreness deepening into a soft and welcome ache. He brushed his fingers against one of them, hissing at the sensitivity of his skin, like an echo of the strike that had left the bruise there.

His shirt was nowhere to be found, but there was a sleeveless white undershirt—in his size—in the drawer where he'd found the pajama pants. He pulled it on gingerly over tender skin and padded into the hallway on tiptoes.

Everything was quiet. The blinds were down, and the kitchen light was off. Umber must still be sleeping. That was unusual; he wasn't a late sleeper. On silent feet, Nick made his way to Umber's bedroom. A stab of longing went through him. He wanted badly to crawl into bed beside him. He tried to shake off that want. What he had here, it was the best he could hope for, and he wasn't about to ruin it with sentimental bullshit.

Sentimental bullshit like having your top stroke your hair until you fall asleep? He couldn't quite tell if his internal voice was being cynical or hopeful. Probably both.

Umber's door was half-open. Nick slid into the bedroom, giving his eyes a moment to adjust to the deeper darkness. There were no windows in Umber's master bedroom, and that was how he liked it, a little sanctuary of night even when the sun was blazing. After a moment, Nick's eyes adjusted enough that he could see Umber. He was propped up in bed between two pillows, snoring very gently, one hand resting against his chest.

Something seemed to expand inside his chest until it almost hurt to breathe. He stood still in the center of the room, just watching for a moment. Then he cleared his throat, softly enough that if Umber was deeply asleep, he'd, hopefully, remain so.

His eyes opened. He blinked twice, and then he focused on Nick. His face shifted from neutral into an easy, sleepy smile. "Nick," he said, voice a little hoarse with sleep. "Would you like to come and join me?"

"If you would like," he said, suddenly shy,

Umber shifted one of the pillows he was propped up against and laid it down, patting it to show there was room for Nick beside him.

Nick slid into bed. The sheets were silky and warm with Umber's presence. Umber lifted his arm slightly so Nick could slot underneath it, cheek laid against his chest. He let out a satisfied sigh and settled in, warm against the flannel of Umber's pajamas. Umber curled the arm around Nick's shoulders and squeezed slightly, affirming his place there.

For a few minutes, they were silent. The only sound was their mingled breathing and the calm lub-dub of Umber's heartbeat flush against Nick's ear.

"You must be exhausted," Nick finally said.

"I am," Umber admitted. "But it is worth the exhaustion." He laughed softly, his breath stirring Nick's hair. "Today you may take care of me while I lounge in bed."

Nick closed his eyes. *I don't want to leave.* The thought was bittersweet, an awareness that eventually he would have to. Leave the bed, leave Umber's apartment. To leave Umber, in the end. Eventually, all good things came to an end, didn't they?

Not right now, though. *Right now, I don't have to go anywhere.*

As if reading his mind, Umber drew him in closer, his lips brushing the top of Nick's head. After a while, Nick turned himself slightly so he could see Umber's face. "Hey, so who's your friend in San Francisco?"

"Hm?" Umber seemed confused for a moment—it was a rare enough look on his face that Nick almost cherished it.

"When we—when we started this, you said you had a friend in San Francisco who you could try and get me a job with." He smiled. "You know, in case I wanted to run so far away from you I'd need to get across the country."

"A correspondent," Umber said. "Not quite a friend."

No—I'm not sure you actually have any of those. It was a little sad, but no less sad than he had been. Who did he count as a friend, these days? Alex? The few army buddies he'd kept in touch with, who he spoke to maybe twice a year? "All right," he said, "who's your correspondent?"

"We've never met face to face," Umber said.

"So he's an internet friend." Nick grinned. "You know, when I first met you, I thought you were a complete technophobe. The kind of guy who wouldn't know what to do with a computer if it bit him."

"Really?" Umber seemed amused. "Perhaps that was intentional. Perhaps it suits me to portray the bumbling Luddite."

"Does it?"

"It does lend a certain authenticity to the image of the antiques dealer, doesn't it?"

"You make it sound like you're just faking being an antiques dealer."

He was quiet a moment. "Her name is Elly Pryce. My friend in San Francisco. We met on a message board for trans people with chronic illnesses."

"Huh. That sounds pretty niche."

"You'd be surprised," he said dryly. "Miss Pryce and I both have fibromyalgia, and have some other... intersecting interests. We became regular correspondents, trading information and, yes, becoming friends."

"Did you...you know..."

"No, Nick, I do not know. What do you mean?"

"Have a thing for her?"

"No, I'm afraid that despite some mutual interests, Miss Pryce and I would be entirely incompatible. I prefer men, you see."

"So," Nick said after a while, "you weren't going to send me to someone you thought I was better suited to."

"If you left because you were offended by my presumption, I would hardly send you to someone else who might presume the same."

He shrugged against Umber's chest. "I just—wanted to hear it."

Umber's hand tangled in his hair—pulled his head back in a gesture perfectly poised between gentle and rough. "Wanted to hear that I want you all for myself?"

Nick gasped. "Yes."

He held him there a little while longer, his eyes amused, considering. "If I was not as exhausted as I am," he said, releasing Nick, "I would show you exactly how much I want you for myself, Nick."

"You do," Nick said softly. "You are."

Umber's face softened. "Come here."

They kissed. It was slow, gentle, closed-mouth. There was no heat to it, no spark of lust, but a kind of sweet desire Nick could simply dissolve into.

Umber pulled away slowly with a regretful sigh. "Go and make breakfast, Nick. I would like to take it in bed today."

"Yes, Mr. Umber." He started to move away.

"Nick? Wait."

He held still for a moment.

"I am...a private man," Umber said. "As you have gathered. It is not always easy for me to share my life with someone. That is why I delayed so long in hiring a PA, relying on piecemeal services."

He seemed to be hesitating—faltering, almost. Nick's heart felt painfully large within him, full of warmth, full of—

Love. The realization had been there, waiting just under the surface. *I love him.* It would have terrified him to think that, a few weeks ago. Now it seemed somehow like the most natural thing in the world.

"What I am trying to say," Umber went on, "is that I want...more of you. In my life. Perhaps, if you would not mind, you could spend a few evenings here every week. The guest room is always available to you. On some nights, I may ask you to share my bed. If that would be acceptable to you."

"Yes, Mr. Umber." His throat was scratchy with something that seemed like the threat of tears, but he managed to keep his voice steady. "I would like that. A lot."

"Then it's settled."

"You can ask me to stay," Nick said. "Anytime you want."

"As can you, Nick," he said—he reminded him. "I like it when you ask me for things. Especially if I can give them to you."

Nick grinned. "Then let me ask you what you'd like for breakfast."

"Can you make eggs Benedict?"

"For you, Mr. Umber, I'll damn well try."

*

When Nick entered the coffee shop, he scanned around automatically for familiar faces. He'd met Gordon in here a few more times, striking up something like a friendship, and brought Alex after his last breakup left him slightly leery of meeting up at the Hellhole. Really should introduce those two, sometime, he thought. They'd never work as lovers, but they might make good friends.

It was funny; he'd been dodging anything like friendship for months—years? Ever since his mother and Lily had died, he guessed. Alex had fought his way in through sheer, stubborn persistence, but even Alex he held at a distance. Now he invited people out, looked for them—not to dodge their company but because it would be a pleasure to see them. Something had loosened in him, and he knew what—who—to thank for it. He shuffled up the line, smiling to himself. *I'll have to make sure that I do, then.*

"Mr. Kurosawa! Nick!" The voice was familiar, though he couldn't quite place it. When he turned around, he had a moment of blankness about the face, as well, until its components—blonde pixie cut, blue eyes behind glasses—clicked into place in his memory.

"Agent Marks. You're still in Westerley?"

She showed her crooked grin. "Still chasing after your boss. He hasn't returned my messages."

"I'll remind him again when I see him."

"Thanks. I'm off the clock right now, though, so you can drop the 'agent' and just call me Siobhan." She tilted her head toward the board. "What's good here?"

"Try the coconut milk latte," he said. "Sounded a bit odd to me when I first tried it, but it's honestly really good."

"Thank you." She sidled herself in ahead of him in the line. "Two coconut milk lattes, please? One medium, one large." She grinned back over her shoulder. "The large one's for you."

"I should really refuse," he said.

"That's what someone who's not gonna refuse would say."

A vague regional accent crept in around the edges of her words—he couldn't quite place it. Maybe Bostonian? He made a note to ask her where she was from. "All right," he said. "But the next one is on me."

It was almost a flirtation, except he was pretty sure Siobhan was a lesbian, and that she knew he was gay. It was an instinct he had, more than anything specific about her. So, a kind of flirtation, really. The kind you did when you were queer in hostile territory, and trying to make friends.

They took their coconut lattes and found a seat toward the back of the cafe. Sedate, folk-inflected pop played over the speakers, blurring with the hubbub of the other patrons—that pleasant, coffee-shop buzz. Siobhan brought four packets of sugar to the table and offered him two. He shook his head.

"You should try it before you put sugar in," he said. "It's sweet enough with the coconut milk."

She snorted. "Doubt it'll be sweet enough for me, but all right." She took a sip, then made a face. "Nah. Gotta have the sugar." She ripped open a packet with her teeth and dumped it into her coffee.

"Better?"

She took another sip. "Much."

"So, hey, thanks for the coffee." He lifted it up, as if to make a toast. "Is this all prelude to you buttering me up for information about my boss?"

"Why, you have some information for me?" she teased, then shook her head. "Like I said, I'm off the clock. Believe it or not, even FBI agents get days off."

"You're still stuck in Westerley though."

"Unfortunately the case." She lifted her coffee, a mirrored tribute. "At least I have company."

"Hear, hear."

They sipped at their lattes. The folk-pop changed to a twangy bluegrass song.

"So correct me if I'm wrong," Siobhan said, "but you're not from Westerley, are you?"

He laughed. "God, no. Born and raised in Hawaii. Oahu, I mean, not the big island."

"Hawaii?" She whistled between her teeth; she was good at it. "Why the heck would you leave paradise to come to a place like this. Uh, no offense to the locals, or anything."

His laughter faded to a small smile. "You ever been to Hawaii?"

"I wish!"

"It's beautiful," he said, "but it's not paradise. Unless you're a rich tourist, I guess. Or maybe a surfer living out of the back of his van. The cost of living is sky-high, and that's just an island thing. And..." He shrugged. "It can be pretty provincial. I guess that's an island thing too."

"All right, but why Westerley? If you're looking to get away from provincial."

"Cheap housing, mostly. I've been thinking about moving since pretty much the moment I got here, but I've got a decent place at a steal."

"Do you miss Hawaii?"

"I don't know." He shrugged again. "Whatever else it is, it's still home. How about you? Where are you from?"

"Rhode Island, originally, but I haven't been back for a while." Her mouth twisted eloquently. "Family, you know how it gets."

"I know how it gets," he agreed softly. He'd been lucky with his mom and dad, but he was thinking of Aunt Fiona.

"So, after Quantico, I just went were the Bureau sent me. Bit of a nomad that way, I guess. Home's Washington, at the moment, but it could be Omaha tomorrow. Though I hope not."

"Nobody special in your life?"

She grinned crookedly. "Not at the moment. One or two girlfriends along the way. How about you?"

He smiled—*Knew it.* "There's a guy I'm seeing. He's—he's the first one for a while. We'll see where it goes though."

"Well, good luck with him." She leaned in closer. "Westerley doesn't have much of a queer scene, does it?"

"Not really. I used to doorman for the Hellhole on Victoria Avenue, and that's the only gay bar we've got. They've got a women's night every other Thursday."

"Every other Thursday?" She rolled her eyes. "Amazing."

"Well, you have to keep yourself busy somehow while looking into my boss."

Her smile faded. "Not really your boss I'm looking into, but unfortunately, the person I really want to speak to is dead."

"Margaret Mason, huh? What did she do?"

"Well, that's the thing." She leaned back in her hair and crossed her ankles. "Probably nothing. I'm chasing a cold case."

"You allowed to talk about it?"

"You want to hear?"

He raised his eyebrows. "Sure, why wouldn't I?"

"Most people glaze over when they realize my job isn't quite being Agent Scully," she said. "I'm not tracking down aliens. Or even terrorists. I'm just...a glorified cop on an old robbery case, basically."

"Sounds pretty interesting to me."

"Well..." She leaned forward to pick up her coffee again, and something in her face seemed to click into a different expression—suddenly serious.

On the clock again, he thought.

"Fifteen years ago, there was a string of thefts from very high-value targets. Corporate theft, mostly, although some high-profile robberies of individual targets have also been linked to the same MO." She paused. "I know this might sound a little too complimentary of criminals, but these were perfectly executed thefts, really. Part hacking, part social engineering, part sheer ballsiness, and barely a scrap of evidence left. You always hear about the perfect crime, but it's rare you actually see it in the wild. Most people get sloppy at some point. The person, or people, responsible for these thefts never did. We estimate they walked away with roughly sixty-eight million dollars in total."

Nick whistled between his teeth. "That's not pocket change."

"No, it isn't. That sort of money is also hard to launder completely. Although they did a fine job at it, the FBI and FinCEN did manage to trace some transactions. My predecessors on the case followed them up, but most of them led into blind alleys. Then, well...then it landed in my lap, and it fell to me to tie up the loose ends."

"And this is what, your last loose end?"

She dumped another packet of sugar into her coffee and stirred it vigorously. "About thirteen years ago, Margaret Mason received a deposit into her bank account from a shell company registered in Singapore—a company that had come into existence a few months after the last known activity of our suspect or suspects, and which seems to have gone up in smoke only days after Ms. Mason's windfall."

"You think Margaret Mason was—?"

"Seems unlikely, I know. She wasn't the only one to receive a deposit from this company, but most of those deposits trickled out of the accounts again before those people even seemed to notice they were there. Ms. Mason, though, well, she seemed to have kept her share of the money."

Nick frowned. "You think Mr. Umber has something to do with this? As far as I know, he never even met Margaret Mason."

She spread her hands. "I'm following up my last lead, Nick, that's all. It's not like I can raise Ms. Mason from the dead and ask her."

His heart was suddenly beating uncomfortably fast. That amount of money would set anyone up for life. For a new life, if they knew how to make it happen. "You sure you're not barking up the wrong tree?" he asked, hoping he managed to sound casual.

She shrugged. "Of course I'm not sure. But it's the one I've got to bark up." She downed the rest of her coffee and made a face. "This is a lot better hot. Guess I let time get away from me a bit, huh? Sorry if I bored you."

He shook his head. "You didn't bore me."

"Well, you're one in a million, Nick." She stood up and squeezed his shoulder companionably. "Tell your boss to give me a call, all right? The sooner I can get out of Westerley, the better."

"If you promise one more coffee before you go."

She laughed. "All right, it's a promise."

*

He found Umber in his office, behind his slab of a desk. A myriad of windows were open on his dual monitors, each one of them an impenetrable wall of text or numbers. When Nick entered, the screens went dark, and Umber turned around in his office chair with a vague smile— which dropped once he saw the expression on Nick's face.

"Are you all right?"

The tone of concern in his voice was so endearingly sincere Nick almost fell right into the trap; it would have been so easy to kneel, now, to lay his head in Umber's lap and let him soothe all Nick's worries away. Instead, he took a shuddering breath and sighed. "So I had coffee with Agent Marks today."

There was a slight seismic shift in Umber's eyebrows, but he said nothing.

Nick went on. "She talked a little about the case she's on, and why she wants to talk to you. She's mostly interested in what you know about Margaret Mason, but... One or two things she said had me wondering."

"Wondering," Umber echoed.

Nick sighed again. "I'm not—I'm not stupid."

"Indeed not," Umber said.

"I help run your shop. I know it's basically a hobby for you. Unless you're selling some ancient artifacts under the table. And you can't make a lot of money doing...whatever else you do, because that's basically charity."

"You are asking me to get into the particulars of my financial affairs?"

Nick resisted the urge to roll his eyes. "I'm asking if I'm right, Mr. Umber."

"All right." There was a long silence then. Umber half turned away from him, looking into the middle distance. "What if I told you—"

Nick let him work through whatever was stopping his words, even though his heart was beating palpably in his throat.

"What if I told you that I am not, exactly, who I presented myself to be."

Nick breathed out. There wasn't exactly a question mark in Umber's words. It was closer to a confession than a question. "I kind of got that idea," he said, his voice desert-dry.

Umber's mouth quirked. "That's the problem with inviting someone clever and observant into your life, I suppose."

"Stop the flattery and get to the point," Nick said. The words were harsh, but he didn't feel anger—only a queer sense of relief, like something that had been held over his head too long had finally fallen.

"You must have guessed already." Umber snorted a laugh. "Agent Marks might, at the moment, think she is investigating Margaret Mason, but she is in truth investigating me."

"You stole over sixty million dollars."

Umber sighed and sat down, leaving Nick standing; feeling like he was looming over him. Maybe that was intentional. "Yes, I was a thief, Mr. Kurosawa. A good enough one I didn't get caught."

"That's a hell of a way to summarize a legendary criminal career," Nick deadpanned.

"To be legendary requires you to be known. I made sure I wasn't. It was...a long time ago."

Nick squatted in front of Umber's chair, looking up at him. "Tell me about it." He hesitated for a moment, then laid a hand on Umber's thigh. "Please?"

He laughed hollowly. "Why, Mr. Kurosawa? It's ancient history. The only relevant information is that your employer is a criminal."

He drew his hand away. "My employer?"

"You know what I mean."

"No, I don't." Nick turned away, not wanting Umber to see his eyes glassing over with unshed tears. "I fucking don't. Is that all I am to you, just...just your bought and paid for assistance dog?"

"You're worrying about the wrong things." Umber's voice was strangely gentle. "But, all right. I'll tell you." He sighed and looked over Nick's shoulder, into a dim and distant past. "After my parents died, I was taken into care. For...one reason and another, I left it as promptly as I could. Afterward, well." His mouth quirked in a humorless smile. "You will never believe how easy it is for someone already branded a deviant and freak to fall in with criminals."

"I've got some idea," Nick said softly.

"Hmph." It was a soft, huffing noise, but in response, Umber tentatively reached out to him, stroking his thumb along the edge of Nick's cheekbone.

Nick wanted nothing more than to melt into his touch, but he kept himself steady. "All right. Go on."

"It was the early days of the Internet. A little more Wild West than it is today. I fell in with, well, extralegal types."

"Extralegal types," Nick echoed.

Umber raised an eyebrow. "Yes. Hackers, con men, phreakers. Many of us had...grievances, whether legitimate or not. We saw what we did as...taking from the man, to survive. Eventually, it seemed natural to move toward more ambitious aims."

"Aims like stealing over sixty million dollars from a bunch of filthy rich folks."

"At the time, I saw it as income redistribution."

"I don't see you giving your wealth to the poor."

"Not all of it." The half smile flickered temporarily into full bloom. "I will grant you that. I became used to the...the freedom of money, I suppose. To live where I wanted. To dress how I wanted. To be able to stop jumping through hoops all the time."

Nick remembered the woman in the run-down apartment, clutching Umber's envelope to her chest with murmured prayers. "But you do help people."

"I still use my wealth and my skills, sometimes, to assist where the law can't. Erasing a troublesome past that keeps tracking someone down. Providing a passport when one's asylum case has been denied." He shrugged. "Perhaps I still take foolish risks, now and then."

"How does Margaret Mason fit into it, though? The store?"

"Maggie..." He shook his head. "It was stupid, I know. I thought I'd gotten away with it. Maggie Mason showed me kindness, once. When I was a runaway foster child, looking queer as a three-dollar bill and with bruises on my face and knuckles, I ended up in Westerley. On my way to California," he said, with faint wistful air, "if you can believe that. I think whatever coast you're born on, you have this...innate feeling that escape is only possible on its opposite. Do you know what I mean?"

"Nope," Nick said. "I'm an island boy. Both coasts seemed equally far to me."

"Hah. Fair..." He looked away again. "Maggie took me in when it would have been wiser to leave me on the street. I stayed with her for a few weeks, and then I was on my way, but I always remembered her. When I came into my fortune, I started...slipping her some money, now and then. She never knew where it was from—and never seemed to spend it either. The last was...I don't know. I was trying for a grand gesture, perhaps, to spur her to some long-delayed retirement."

He was silent a moment. "When she died, I didn't want the store to go to someone who would sell it and gut it. It's never exactly been profitable, you know."

"All right." Nick was frowning. "I get the feeling that was the very quick and dirty version of things."

"Admittedly."

"So." He took a deep breath. "Now what?"

"Now what?" Umber made a movement that wasn't a shrug as much as a cringe. "When your cover is compromised, it must be exchanged for another."

"And that's what you're planning to do."

Umber was quiet for what seemed like a very long time. "I would advise you to call Agent Marks tomorrow and tell her...whatever you'd like. But don't allow yourself to be looked at as an accomplice."

"Why tomorrow?"

"Because..." Umber's eyes were dry, but horribly empty. He looked like a man facing a firing squad. "Because I think you will want to attempt to shield me, and if you wait until tomorrow, then I will have had the time to put my contingency plan in action. If you call tonight, now, then I will wait here until they come to arrest me. You may wait with me, to ensure it."

"You'd do that?"

He nodded.

Nick put his hand on Umber's cheek. He closed his eyes and leaned into the touch, suppressing a groan as Nick touched him. "If you think I'm letting you vanish into the night," Nick said, surprising himself with the steadiness of his own voice, "you don't know me as well as I thought you did." He grinned. "Vanishing into the night includes being dragged to jail."

"Mr. Kurosawa...Nick..." He swallowed and closed his hand over Nick's, dragging their linked fingers down into his lap. "I cannot ask this of you."

"But I can offer." He held Umber's hand tightly, not letting him draw away again. "This contingency plan, it involves vanishing, doesn't it?"

He nodded slowly.

"You've done it before, haven't you?"

"Yes." His voice was soft.

"A little over ten years ago. How bad was your fibro, then?"

Umber narrowed his eyes. *Good, if you're irritated, you won't sit there feeling sorry for yourself. Be practical, Mr. Umber, even if it annoys you.* "Not as bad as it is today. What exactly is your point?"

"Just that you could use your assistance dog."

"You're not—"

"I know," Nick said, cutting him off. "It's a joke, Mr. Umber. I'm still allowed to make those."

"You can't do this for me, Nick. Please, I don't want you to ruin your life for the mistakes I made." He laughed humorlessly. "Am still making."

"Look. This place isn't bugged, right?"

Umber looked vaguely affronted. "Of course not. I make sure of that."

"Say it all goes to hell, and you get caught. As far as Agent Marks, the FBI, the cops, whatever, know...you're my employer. You tell me to drive you out of state, for example, I drive you out of state. Why the hell would I question it? You ask me to do enough weird shit."

Umber stroked the back of his hand. "But say it all works just as planned," he said after a while. "Say I vanish and take you with me. You'd lose everything—your entire life, your name, your identity. It isn't worth it."

Nick was silent. It wasn't that he didn't know how to answer. It was that he wasn't sure Umber wanted to hear it. "I don't know much about your past," he said. "And maybe I don't need to, not really. But you know everything about mine." He wanted Umber to remember the file, maybe half an inch thick, with all his paltry secrets laid bare. "You know I don't have much to leave behind."

"Not having very much," Umber said, "sometimes means what remains is defended all the more fiercely. As it should, perhaps."

"There is something I don't want to leave behind," Nick said in a small voice. He looked sideways at Umber, not wanting to complete the thought, knowing he was smart enough to know what he meant.

"Oh, Nick..."

"It's your choice." His voice was harsh. "It's always your choice."

"Do you really know what you're offering?"

"You ask that every time I offer something," Nick said. "I'm not a child, and I'm not an idiot. And you can't know every possible outcome, either, you know."

Umber reached for him, cradling his cheek. This time, Nick allowed himself to melt into his touch.

"No," Umber said softly and leaned in to kiss him. "I don't suppose I can."

Part Four

DEPARTURES

Nick swung the car into the motel parking lot. The vacancy sign blinked a bleary neon-green. It reminded him of the neon around the Hellhole, lighting up the colors of Umber's tie. Vacancy was right, there were maybe three cars in the lot. The windows of the cabins were dark, but there was a wan yellow light on in the office.

"Wait in the car," he told Umber. "I'll be right back."

The night air was cool but not cold. The farther West they drove, the more congenial the climate became, if by slow degrees. For a moment, he glanced back at Umber, half hidden behind the tinted windows of the old Toyota.

The car had been bought with cash from a used-car lot near the outskirts of Westerley. Once they'd decided to move, they moved fast. Nick had left a message for Alex, saying he'd be out of town a few days. He'd felt a twinge of guilt, at that. Alex deserved better—even Gordon deserved not to be ghosted. He'd have to figure it out as he went. All he knew for sure was that he couldn't let Umber do this alone.

He crossed the empty parking lot and went into the office. A tired, dark-eyed woman sat in the office behind a shield of thick glass, perforated with a circle of holes at mouth-level, like a bank-teller's window. "How can I help you?" she asked.

"I'd like a room for the night."

"We take cash in advance, and I'll need to see your driver's license."

He took the license from his wallet. The picture was him, looking grim and washed-out, the name Takeshi Anderton. ("Randomly generated," Umber had told him. "If we need something that would hold up to more robust scrutiny, we may have to rethink.") Nick's heart was in his throat; he was sure she'd notice something amiss. Umber had printed it last night, before pouring acid on his computers.

Nothing happened. She wrote down his information, name and license number, in a fat and dog-eared ledger, and then handed it back without another word. He paid for the room, and she slid across a key, attached to an immense wooden keyring in the shape of a cowboy hat, the paint decorating it long faded. It had 2B printed on it in black ink, gone over again and again with permanent marker.

Umber hadn't moved from his spot in the passenger seat. He was staring ahead into nothing, his eyes reflecting the flickering neon of the vacancy sign. He looked bone-tired. A sudden surge of emotion threatened to close Nick's throat, a mix of frustration and affection so intense it almost hurt. He stopped about ten paces from the car, looking at Umber. Trying to get back to something like neutral.

After a while, he gave up on that idea and just knocked on the window. Umber turned his head slowly, blinking up at him as if he barely recognized him. "We've got a room."

He unlocked the door and started to get out. Nick held out his hand. Umber looked at it as if he didn't quite understand it, then finally reached out and took it, letting Nick haul him to his feet. "Thank you, Mr. Kurosawa," he said, his voice soft.

"Here's the key." he said, pressing it into Umber's hand. "We're in 2B. I'll get your bag."

He went to the trunk and got out Umber's black shoulder bag, the one they'd packed his medication in. He wondered how many days' worth was in there, and how they would get more. Worse come to worst, they could always ram-raid a pharmacy, he thought, and half laughed. The fucked-up thing was, it sounded like a plausible plan.

Headlights cut across the dark parking lot, and his head shot up, his heart pounding again—but it was just a beat-up pickup truck with a bearded man at the steering wheel. Nick was fairly sure they hadn't been followed, but still...

He sighed and ran a hand through his hair. He wasn't as tired as Umber looked, but it had been a damned long day. He went to the door of 2B and knocked softly. There was a click of a lock, and Umber let him in.

It was a motel room like any other, as if it had been printed off an assembly line. Double bed; ancient CRT TV on a big, ugly cabinet; a cramped bathroom with a pink plastic shower curtain around the claw-foot tub. He put the bag onto the bed.

"If we leave at eight AM tomorrow," Umber said, "we should be at our next planned stop by sundown."

"I think you need more sleep than...what, six hours?"

"It might be a luxury we cannot afford."

"We weren't followed."

"As far as we are aware."

"All right, yeah. But we can only go off what we know." He took a long, shuddering breath.

"Mr. Kurosawa…" Umber seemed to be struggling for words. "You needn't come with me. When I must go tomorrow."

"I know." It came out harsher than he intended. "I know," he repeated, more softly now. "You can stop giving me outs I never asked for, Jacob. Or…whatever your name is."

"What would you consider to be my real name, Mr. Kurosawa?" His voice had gone chill and soft, and Nick almost wanted to cheer at the show of anger, however mild it might be. "The one I was born with, perhaps?"

"No. The one you call yourself, in your own head. I want to get to call you that."

He was silent for a moment, after that. "Names are…complicated, for me."

"Could just call you sir," Nick offered.

Umber made a sound that could have been a laugh. Nick took a step forward, then another, until he was standing within kissing distance. Then, he went to his knees.

"Oh." Umber stood stock-still, his hands frozen at his sides. "I hardly think I deserve this kind of…I don't deserve this, Mr. Kurosawa. Not after what I've pulled you into."

"Nick," he corrected firmly. He put his hands behind his back and looked up at Umber. "Everything in my life just got extremely complicated, Mr. Umber. Please, just, let me have—let me have one thing that makes sense. Let me have one thing that feels like home."

Umber swallowed. "I don't know if I can keep… standing up."

Nick offered his hand, quick as a flash, and—still kneeling—helped Umber to sit down on the edge of the bed. Then, he laid his head down on Umber's lap.

After a while, Umber started stroking his hair. At first it was hesitant, as if Nick were a dog that might snap at him. Then, slowly, the touch became more confident. Nick let out a rumbling, pleased sound and allowed himself to melt under Umber's touch, forgetting everything except his place at Umber's knee.

About ten minutes later, Umber stroked the back of Nick's neck and said, "Nick? Would you please find us both some food?"

Nick got up, slower than usual; his legs still ached from the long drive. "Of course," he said, smiling down at Umber. "I can't promise it'll be anything good at this time of night in the middle of nowhere."

"A chocolate bar and a bag of chips from a vending machine would be just fine. Just something to get some calories into us, that's all."

"That I can do."

He managed to do better than that. The vending machine in the office was the kind that dispensed sandwiches. He got two cheese sandwiches and two decaf coffees as well as a candy bar to share, and brought them to Umber. He sat on the floor, leaning against the bed, while they ate, and Umber sat on the edge of the bed, with one leg swung over Nick's shoulder.

There was something strangely smug in Nick's contentment, sitting like this. He knew it was stupid. It was three in the morning, they were in a mediocre motel somewhere in a reception dead zone (Nick wasn't even sure what state they were in), they were very possibly fugitives from the FBI—or at least Umber was, though he supposed he counted as an accessory—and he'd just driven across state lines (probably) with a fake driver's license. Smug wasn't the appropriate emotion. Fear, maybe, and some of that anger that had flared in him earlier. He searched himself for it and found neither. He was too tired to be afraid, and too...

Too home. When I am with him, I am home.

*

"Nick? Can you help me bathe?" Umber's voice had a catch to it Nick hadn't heard before, a weary vulnerability. "I'm...I'm very tired right now."

Nick got to his feet and threw the empty sandwich packet into the trash with a perfect arc. "I'll run a bath."

"I mean." He swallowed. "Actually help me."

Nick nodded. "Of course."

He ran the bath. They didn't have Umber's Epsom salts and essential oils, but Nick made do with the bath soap the motel provided, working the anemic suds up into a respectable soapy foam with his hand. Then he knelt in front of the bed again and untied Umber's shoes. He took them off and put them aside as Umber unbuttoned his shirt. There was nothing erotic in it, it wasn't a striptease to say the least, but Nick still got a warm rush of desire when Umber's shirt fell away, and he was sitting there in trousers and white undershirt, his shoulders bare.

"Would you like me to undo your belt?" he asked. His voice was very low.

"No," Umber said, "I can manage. Can—can you help pull off my trousers?"

Nick inclined his head in acknowledgment and slid Umber's trousers down, over his hips and off. He wore black silk boxers. Somehow, it surprised Nick; he was half expecting starched white briefs. "Would it help if I took my own clothes off?" he asked, not quite joking.

Umber smiled. "You might want to strip down to what you won't mind getting wet, but otherwise, no, that's quite all right."

He turned around, giving Umber a moment's privacy while he stripped off his undershirt and boxers. He took off his jeans and his shirt, leaving himself in what Umber had just taken off—white undershirt and black boxers, though his were a faded cotton instead of midnight-colored silk.

"Give me your arm, please?"

He did. He led Umber to the bathroom, trying to ignore the urge to look at him. He wanted to drink in the sight of him, but he was too keenly aware that it wasn't Umber's choice that led him to finally show his body, but necessity. He helped him into the bathtub, only looking back at him when the suds had covered him from toes to sternum.

There was a stack of washcloths, a little grayed and ragged but clean, and he took one and soaked it in the soapy water. "May I?"

"Please."

He started to wash Umber, gently massaging him until he laid his head back against the lip of the tub and closed his eyes. Faint, amber-red light leaked through the high window; it was nearly sunrise. "We should sleep as long as we can," Nick said softly. "If your itinerary can allow it, we'll both be better off with some extra rest."

"You're right," Umber said. "And I fear I may not have a choice, despite the itinerary I planned." His head lolled against the edge of the bath, his eyes distant and unfocused.

They were both silent for a moment.

"Shall I...rinse you off?"

"No, just hand me the showerhead."

He did, and turned away, getting a towel ready while Umber rinsed himself off.

"Help me out of the bath?"

He did, and handed him the towel, looking into the middle distance over Umber's shoulder. If he didn't want Nick to see him naked—if this was out of necessity, and not out of want—then he simply...wouldn't look.

He was startled by Umber's hand on his cheek. Umber looked at him, skin still watery-slick, hair plastered down and even darker than usual. "Nick," he said, a world of fondness in his voice. He said Nick's name as if it were a precious thing.

They kissed. Neither of them began it. They came together like they were following the steps of a dance. Nick moaned, low and soft, and Umber cradled the back of his neck, pulling him deeper into the kiss. He was hard against Umber's wet, naked body, his undershirt and boxers soaked through. He let himself hold him, let his hands slide against the damp skin of his back. Umber's muscles shifted under his hands as he pressed himself closer to Nick.

They broke the kiss. Umber smiled up at him. "If I was less tired, I'd make sure you were properly taken care of."

"You don't—you don't need to do anything."

"I know," he said. "But I want to."

Nick swallowed. When he spoke, his voice was low and husky. "Yeah. Me too."

"Nick." Umber shifted, parting his legs slightly. "Would you like to touch me?"

He made a helpless, incoherent noise and slid a hand between Umber's legs. He was hard and slick and very hot. Nick slid two fingers on either side of Umber's cock and rested them there, feeling the urgent beat of his heart.

Umber closed his eyes and let his head rest against Nick's shoulder as Nick stroked him. He wanted more, wanted to go to his knees and suck him, wanted to slide his fingers into Umber and feel his heartbeat from the inside. But it would be too fast, too much. This, this slow touch, this indulgence, with both of them dead-tired and wet and needing sleep more than sex. This was what they had, and he was going to enjoy every moment of it.

Umber's cock twitched under his fingers. He rocked his hips and let out a sound that was nearly a growl, his mouth pressed hard against Nick's shoulder. Then a full-body shiver went through him, and he sagged against Nick, limp and shivering. When his knees went weak, Nick was there to catch him.

He picked him up with a grunt of effort—Umber might have been a head shorter than him, but he was solidly built—and carried him out of the bathroom. He laid him down on the bed. Umber reached out and stroked his damp hair, something infinitely tender in his gaze. "Thank you," he said. "For everything. For being who you are."

Nick suddenly felt as if he were about to cry. He buried his face in the curve of Umber's hip, pressing it against warm skin, breathing in the scent of him. "I love you," he murmured against Umber's skin, almost not loud enough to be heard.

Almost.

Umber stiffened ever so slightly, then let himself relax. His grip on Nick's hair tightened. "And I you," he said slowly, as if he were just coming to terms with the idea. "Nick..."

Nick raised his head. "Where do you—where do you want me tonight?"

Umber kept his grip on Nick's hair, raising his head ever so slightly so that he could look into Nick's eyes. In the dusky light his storm-green eyes looked black. "Where do you want to be?"

A desperate emptiness had opened up in Nick's chest, a black hole he could not explain. It was as if nothing that Umber could give him would be enough to sate him. He made a sound in the back of his throat, a low, laughing whimper. "I don't know," he said.

Umber was silent for a long while. Nick could hear his own heart beating in his ears. He wondered if Umber had fallen asleep.

"Sleep here with me," Umber finally said. "Please?"

Nick slunk up beside him and let himself be held. Umber was warm and strong beside him. Nick let out a long, shuddering breath. It wasn't enough to fill that strange void in him, but, God, it was good. Umber's arms wrapped tight around him, stroking him until exhaustion overwhelmed the chaos of emotions in him—the joy, the fear, the aching need—and he fell asleep.

*

When Nick woke up the bed was empty and cold. He sat up, heart hammering. Morning light filtered through the blinds, and Umber's bag was gone. "No," he said, then flinched at the sound of his own voice in the empty room.

He jumped out of bed, not bothering to pull on clothes, and barreled outside. The car was still there, and a spasm of massive relief went through him. Umber couldn't have gone anywhere without the car. He was probably just getting some food, or maps, or—

Yeah. *That's all stuff he needs his entire bag for, isn't it?* Nick shivered in the chill morning air and went back inside the room.

There was a note taped to the television. He hadn't noticed it, in his scrambled, just-awoken dash outside. He pulled it off with a yank so violent it almost toppled the TV. He knew already what it would say—the content, if not the form. Half of him wanted to rip it to pieces without even bothering to read it, but the other, calmer half was still in control.

Dear Nick, he read, and it was enough to undo him. The tears started blurring his vision. He wiped them away with a harsh stroke of his hand, biting into his tongue to stop any more from falling. He'd be damned if he would fall apart now.

> *Dear Nick, I am sorry. You will never know how sorry I am. But if I want to be able to look at myself in the mirror ever again, I cannot drag you into this any further than I already have. I will not sully myself any further by asking for your forgiveness. I know you will see this as unforgivable. I only hope you know that in one respect, at least, I never lied to you.*

It wasn't signed. There was nothing else. He looked at it with a kind of dull emptiness. Once he'd bitten back his tears, he had no feelings left.

He considered ripping it to pieces and leaving it in the trash in this dingy motel room. Maybe even tossing it down the toilet—nothing so dramatic as burning it. But instead, he folded it up very small and tucked it in his wallet, behind the picture of Lily and his cousins.

He got dressed, his movements like those of an automaton slowly running out of charge. He wasn't hungry at all, but he stopped into the office to get a cup of coffee. The woman from last night was gone, replaced by a bored-looking man who grunted vaguely at Nick in greeting.

"You didn't happen to see a guy leaving here, fortyish, dark brown hair, wearing a dark suit?" Nick had to ask.

The man looked at him blearily. "Buddy, that describes about half the guys we get in here."

Nick shrugged and left the office, cup of coffee in hand. It was a cool, clear day. A few furry clouds edged the Eastern sky, but other than that, it was a bright field of blue. He took a sip of his coffee. It was hot and almost tasteless, but he drunk it nonetheless, hoping the caffeine would at least put a little energy in him. It didn't matter, anyway. He could keep going like this, moving his limbs automatically.

He got in the car and opened the glove compartment. It was empty, except for a thick manila envelope. He touched it briefly, felt the bulge of money inside. For a brief moment he was incandescently angry—he wanted to tear that stupid envelope open and toss the bills all over the parking lot, let the traveling salesmen and the cheating husbands and the long-haul truckers fight over a few hundred-dollar bills under the pale late-morning sun. Then he snapped the glove compartment shut, started the car, and drove out of the motel parking lot.

The plan, Umber had told him, was to go West, but Umber had lied. Not that it really mattered—Nick couldn't find him, now. Not a man who'd made a lifetime's vocation out of vanishing. So Nick started the long drive back to Westerley.

He didn't have anywhere else to go.

He still had his apartment; he'd not stayed there for a while, but the rent was paid up, and his landlord hands-off. His bank account still had a healthy balance. Umber had mostly insisted on paying for his...his upkeep, as well as his salary since they'd started their relationship. Their arrangement. Whatever.

Nick tightened his hands on the steering wheel—a manic *hooooonk!* from a car behind him made him aware he'd been weaving over the line, and driving about twenty miles below the speed limit. He let the car pass him (with an "asshole!" shouted from the window), straightened his driving, and brought his speed up to normal, keeping his eyes fixed on the road.

Hell, the way Umber had been paying him, he might even have enough to get out of Westerley, to go further East and see the Atlantic Ocean for the first time, find some security work and a cheap apartment in some right-coast state where nobody knew his name.

Or he supposed he could call Alex, or Gordon, or Agent Marks. The latter, to inform her, maybe, that notorious criminal Jacob Umber, alias half a hundred names, was probably hitching a ride with a long-haul trucker down to Mexico, or up to Canada. Look for the well-dressed guy with the cane haunting truck stops. The highway was blurry; he realized he'd been crying for some time now.

He'd left his cell phone in a garbage can, the SIM card snapped, back in Westerley. There was nobody he could call right now. He was alone in the driver's seat.

The longer he drove, the grayer the sky turned, from sapphire to steel, covering the sun with a wintry haze of clouds. Somewhere between the last two truck stops, he'd stopped crying, and his heart was small and cold inside him, a chip of ice spinning in a dim emptiness.

Wherever Umber had gone, it was nowhere that he could be found, and with the letter he'd left Nick, it was doubtful he'd come back. What had it been? He couldn't look at himself in the mirror? Nick wondered how he could look at himself in the mirror, now, and not see a man who'd been touched, claimed, owned by Jacob Umber.

You're being dramatic. How long were you with him—a few months? He was right, Kurosawa. That's not something you give up your whole life for.

Except that he would have done. There was, Nick knew, such a thing as love at first sight, at first touch. His parents had been high school sweethearts; his father told him once that he knew he was going to marry his mother the night of their first date. Nick had rolled his eyes, in his dismissive preteen way, and said that sounded pretty stupid. When his mother told Lily the same story years later, she'd said, "That's pretty lucky, mama," and wasn't that just Lily all over. A lot nicer and a lot smarter than her brother had ever been.

He thought remembering Lily and his parents would bring the tears back, but whatever had snapped within him had dried them up, even for his family. Well, he'd cried enough tears, more than enough. He'd almost drowned in them. Now, what he needed was to keep driving until he could see Westerley, not waste time pulled over on the side of the road weeping for everything he'd lost.

*

It had seemed impossible that his life and Umber's could be disentangled so easily, but the truth was that it was offensively easy. Whatever bonds they'd forged between them, they had only had a few months—and Umber had always kept him at arm's length, in any case, legally as well as emotionally. Nick understood why, now. Umber had been laying the tracks for his exit before he ever needed to take it. He'd lifted out of Nick's life with ease. The hole he left behind was only in his heart.

The first two nights he'd spent at Alex's. Nick had called him for a pickup after reselling the car back to the same lot (at a significant loss, but who cared? It had been Umber's money). Alex had insisted on feeding and watering Nick through what he called "a tricky breakup," and Nick let him. He wondered if Alex felt guilty for introducing them in the first place. Of course, Alex had thought he was just getting Nick a job interview, not a...whatever they'd had, with a criminal on the run.

On the third day, he'd gone back to his own apartment—Alex would have let him stay longer, but Nick needed space, and privacy—to a stack of unread mail and a ticked-off looking FBI agent on his doorstep.

Siobhan Marks had looked him up and down with a kind of "I'm not mad, just disappointed" air that almost made him laugh. She'd make a hell of a mom. "Hello, Nick."

"Hi, Siobhan. Are you here to arrest me?"

"I probably could, but what the hell for? It's not like you're going to lead me to Jacob Umber, also known as Victor Shade, and another list of aliases about a mile long."

Umber had been right, then—he'd been figured out. "If I knew where he was," he'd said, "I'd probably tell you."

"Probably covers a lot of ground, Nick." She'd shaken her head, hands in her pockets. "Anyway, Umber's assets have been frozen or seized. The ones we could find, anyway. Including Margaret Mason's store. It's a shame. She probably would have preferred it not be torn apart by the government."

"He's not coming back, you know. No use talking to me like he's going to hear what you're saying."

At that, she'd shrugged. "You know my number, Nick. I'll be in touch."

He'd watched her go with something that was almost regret—almost, because there wasn't any room in his heart for it. They could have been friends in another time and place, where she wasn't chasing down the man Nick loved.

He figured he'd keep on loving Umber for a long time. Nick used to think there was something missing in him— that love, real love, was something meant for other people, not for him. But it had come and reconfigured him, nonetheless, and sunk deep roots into his heart. He made himself see it as a hopeful thing. One day, maybe a few years from now, when the wound that Umber had left in his heart had scabbed over, there'd be room in there for someone else. Someone who preferably wasn't a criminal on the run.

Someone who wouldn't leave him.

The money he'd managed to save up would cover a few months' rent and food, if he was frugal. The cash Umber had tried to foist on him, he'd dropped into a mailbox. He'd sent Agent Marks a message telling her where—he figured it was something he owed her. Not that he thought she could track Umber down, but it was the principle of the thing.

Nick knew he should get a job again, maybe call Merritt and offer to pick up any shifts that he needed covering, for one, but something in him held him back. So he went back to his most frugal habits, ramen and tins of soup and cheap crackers, and midnight runs around the block instead of going to the gym.

He also started going to the library nearly every day. At first, he read his way through Westerley's collection of techno-thrillers, then moved on to nonfiction. Thanks to interlibrary loans, he ordered in a whole stack of books he was sure raised a few eyebrows at the collection desk, but he was through being embarrassed.

A good half of the books had been on the list Dr. Flynn had given him a few years back, books that were surprisingly sober and serious despite their often-lurid covers. He found something like kinship between their covers: stories of people who found their home on their knees, or in collars, or performing acts of service for those they judged worthy of it. He wished he'd read them years ago, when he thought it was a choice between a vanilla relationship, if he was even capable of one, and one-off hookups with men he'd hoped would hurt him in the right ways.

He also ordered more practical books. One thing Umber had taught him was that he had a talent for PA work. He already knew he was a good bodyguard. So he read up on navigating the benefits system, as well as concealed carry laws, on the various licensing requirements of a close-protection business, alongside preventing pressure sores. He had a vague notion he could carve out a niche as a care assistant who could also kick ass when needed. And he was willing to bet there were enough disabled folks with abusive exes, or involved in activism that made them targets, to make himself valuable there.

The days ticked by. They turned into weeks. He bought a new phone. He went out for drinks with Alex now and then. Once, he saw Gordon, who raised a glass of beer at him and smiled. He got a letter from the FBI requesting that he notify them if he left the country. He presumed that meant he'd been added to a list of some sort. Not that it mattered very much to him—he wasn't much of a world traveler. He just hoped it wouldn't throw up any wrenches if he wanted to set up his own close-protection business.

Nick was starting to see the shape of a future, dim and uncertain. Had that been thanks to Umber? Before him, there had only been blankness. He signed up with an agency providing emergency care workers—it shocked him, how desperate they were for anyone to take a few shifts—and started working now and then, laying some money by so his savings didn't dwindle to nothing.

He'd just come off a night shift. A paraplegic writer's PA was on holiday, and he'd called the agency to get some cover. Nick had never met the guy before, but they had a good rapport, and he'd spend most of the night drowsing on the couch, summoned to help when needed by a loud alarm on the coffee table. Nick had left after making breakfast, with a warm handshake and the writer's brisk, professional thanks.

He stared up at the brightening sky, arms crossed over his chest. The wind was cool on his face. For a moment, he half closed his eyes. *Maybe I should go out tonight. Call Gordon or Alex, see if they want to have a drink.* It wasn't a want, not exactly—it was just that something in him was nagging that he needed some kind of social life.

He ended up calling Alex that evening, mostly because he came first alphabetically in Nick's pathetically short list of contacts. "Hey."

"Hey, Nick."

"You busy tonight?"

There was a moment's hesitation on Alex's end, and Nick almost hung up on him out of sheer embarrassment—*God, I'm such an asshole for thinking he has nothing better to do.*

But half a second later, Alex said, "Nothing I can't cancel. You want to meet up?"

Nick grimaced. "I don't want you to cancel something if—"

"Oh, stop it, Nick, I wouldn't cancel if I didn't want to. You want to meet at the Hellhole?"

"Anywhere but there, really."

There was another brief moment of silence from Alex's end, but this time Nick didn't think it was hesitation. "Dinner, then. Pizza at Jerry's?"

"Sure." Jerry's was a decent enough place with some quiet booths, and not somewhere Alex would take a date— it'd do fine.

After hanging up, he checked his e-mail. There weren't any assignments from the agency until next week. The day dragged on blankly until dinnertime. Nick tried to read, but couldn't quite focus on the words. After he'd cleaned an already clean apartment, he did sit-ups and push-ups on his living room floor with mindless, mechanical persistence. When his alarm to meet Alex went off, he nearly gasped with relief to have something to do.

It was an early dinner, and Jerry's was near to empty except for a quiet family a few booths down. Alex for once had dressed down in jeans and T-shirt. Nick had, without thinking, thrown on a shirt that Umber had picked out for him.

"You look good," Alex said.

Nick raised an eyebrow, and Alex laughed.

"You do. A little stressed, maybe, but good."

"Thanks, I'll take that." Nick sighed over their plate of breadsticks. "You been up to much?"

Alex nodded. "I've been helping to set up a nonprofit counseling service—just the paperwork. I think they're going to do some good work here. Aubrey, one of the guys who's running it, he's a nice guy, really passionate, and—" Alex looked down at his plate, blushing. "Well. I hope you get to meet him sometime soon."

"I'm glad to hear it," Nick said, meaning it, but after that, his words dried up. He took another breadstick, mostly so his mouth had something to do other than talk. He wondered if Alex had canceled a date with Aubrey to take him out to Jerry's for pizza.

"What about you, Nick?" His voice with gentle. "You looking to start dating again?"

"I've never been much for dating."

Alex shrugged. "Whatever you call it, then."

Nick shook his head. If he could get away with it, he'd cram another breadstick in his mouth—instead, he drank down his cheap white wine and looked out the window, onto the rainy street. He never minded being alone, before Umber. He'd get used to it again sooner or later.

"Maybe you just need a change of scenery." Alex's voice was gentle. "Not that I wouldn't miss you, but..."

"Maybe you're right."

"Yeah, I just might be." Alex seemed to search for words, frowning slightly. "Westerley's always been a—a holding pattern for you, and I think you know it. There are bigger things waiting out there for you, Nick. You just have to go and get them."

He caught Alex's eye and smiled, his first real smile of the evening. "You really believe that, don't you?"

"I really do."

There was a moment's awkward silence between them—then, they both laughed. "Well, I can't go too far," Nick said. "The FBI is still keeping tabs on me, I'm sure."

Alex grimaced. "God! I'm sorry."

He shrugged, grinning. "If you're really sorry, you can buy me another glass of wine."

*

Nick woke up with the ghost of a hangover, the sour taste of bad wine in the back of his throat, and blinked up at the ceiling. There'd been a dream, bittersweet and distant. All he remembered from it now was the feeling of his fingers entwined with another's, fading slowly to the sensation of his hand fisted around the bedsheets. Two seconds later, he realized his phone was vibrating; it had probably been what woke him up in the first place. He took it from the bedside table and saw an unfamiliar number. Even the area code was strange. He frowned, almost letting it go to voice-mail—if it was the FBI again, he wasn't in the mood—but impulsively answered it anyway. "Hello?"

"Am I speaking to Nick Kurosawa?"

The voice was warm, feminine, with a slight ragged edge that struck Nick as oddly familiar, though he'd be willing to bet he'd never heard it before.

"Speaking," he said, propping himself up on his elbow. "How can I help?"

"My name is Elly Pryce. I heard you might be looking for work."

Umber's friend. He was speechless for a moment, then recovered. "Miss Pryce. You're calling from San Francisco?"

"San Rafael, but close enough. I got your number from...a friend."

Nick's throat had gone dry. Umber must have gotten in touch with her—must have fulfilled his promise of months ago. Nick wanted to be angry, but found he couldn't; it felt like his touch on him, from a thousand miles away, and he treasured that too much to be angry at it. "So, to what do I owe the pleasure?" His mouth twitched into a half smile at his word choice. They were Umber's words, almost, like the hint of his presence had awakened some dormant ghost of him in Nick's mind.

"I'll get right to the point." There was something faintly amused in her voice. "I have care needs, and I've been looking to hire a PA in a more permanent capacity. You come highly recommended."

He could not quite repress a bitter huff of a laugh. "Well, whatever you've been told, I've not been doing this work for long. I'm not a nurse, or—"

"I'm not looking for a nurse, Nick."

"Still, Miss Pryce—"

"Elly, please."

"All right. Elly. I'm just not sure if I'm what you're looking for."

"Maybe not," she said. "But I trust"— she gave the word a slight edge —"your references enough to give you a chance nonetheless. I'll cover your travel expenses, and we can have a tryout. If we don't gel—no harm, no foul."

He closed his eyes. *Maybe you just need a change of scenery*, Alex had told him last night. Maybe he'd set him up with this job too. No—Nick knew that if anyone had set him up with Elly Pryce, it was Umber. As a farewell gift, maybe.

"Nick? Are you still there?"

"All right." The words were out of his mouth before he was aware of making the decision. Whatever happened, he could do with seeing the ocean again. "All right. I'll come."

*

Nick stepped off the plane into a warm night. The smell of the air hit him like a wave. He hadn't realized how much he'd missed it until he was there. They were still miles away from the ocean, but he swore he could smell the salt of the Pacific in the air.

He'd packed light, just a carry-on bag. The rest of his things were in storage with Alex. He'd ended the lease on his apartment—whatever happened here, he wasn't going back to Westerley. He'd decided that much. If Elly Pryce didn't work out as an employer, there were other opportunities in California, or Oregon, or, what the hell, back in Hawaii. He could handle the rumors now, stare them dead in the face without shame.

Elly had told him she'd arranged a driver for him—Nick found him holding up a sign saying Nick K in the arrivals lounge. Between that and the all-expenses-paid flight, he wondered if she was as rich as Umber had been, before the FBI had seized his assets anyway. She was one of the fortunate fibro sufferers who could keep their career up, designing software from her home in the hours that the illness left her. One of the very few who could manage to hire a full-time permanent PA.

She'd arranged everything with remarkable speed, but one thing she hadn't done was given him any information about her care needs. Maybe she just preferred discussing it face to face, but it seemed more than a little odd to Nick that she'd hire him sight unseen without so much as a list of what she needed him to do. Just as strange as taking the job without asking, he thought, and snorted a laugh to himself.

"Sorry?" the cab driver said, and Nick shook his head.

"Just thinking out loud."

"No problem, boss, just let me know if there's anything I can do."

He tipped the man well—he could afford to, with Elly Pryce paying his way here—and looked up at her house, a looming monstrosity of a McMansion up a winding, green-fringed drive. Miss Pryce, or Elly as she insisted on being called, had asked that he be dropped off at her gate and walk up the drive after ringing in. He went to the gate, a wrought iron anachronism in the green, and pressed the call button that glowed against iron and brick like an incongruous little moon.

"Who is it?" Elly Pryce's voice was familiar enough from her phone calls.

"This is Nick Kurosawa," he said.

"Come in!" There was real warmth in her voice, even over the intercom. Not for the first time, he wondered how much Umber had told her about him.

The gate slid open, and he started his trek up to the house. The driveway was longer than it seemed, winding itself in serpentine coils up a deceptively steep hill. He hoped Elly didn't have to walk this on a regular basis. If she did, it went more than a little way toward explaining why she didn't go out much.

Finally, he reached the front door. A wheelchair ramp had clearly been added on to it after construction. The door opened, and Elly Pryce grinned at him, leaning on a cane that glittered with the eye-searing shine of half a hundred rhinestones.

She was tall, her back a little stooped, with thick dark hair, and unexpectedly elegant in a jaunty Marlene Dietrich kind of way—somehow, he expected a programmer to look a bit more, well, slovenly.

Shows what I get for making assumptions.

"Hi," she said. "Come in. You must have had a long journey."

He smiled at her and ran a hand through his travel-rumpled hair. "Not that bad. I managed to sleep on the plane."

"Hey, great—listen, come in. We'll have a chat, then depending on how things go, I can call you a taxi back to a hotel for the night, all right?"

Depending on how things go? Nick frowned—what did she think was going to happen here? "Listen, Miss Pryce, just to make things clear, I'm interested in the job you offered me. Nothing more."

A complicated expression passed over her face, and for a moment, Nick was sure she was trying very hard not to laugh. "Have a seat in the living room up front. You want coffee, tea? Something stronger?"

"Coffee might be nice. Hey, you want me to—"

"Not until you're onboarded," she said in a singsong voice, and herded him toward the living room.

It was not as ostentatious as he'd half feared, though it was unquestionably a few ticks higher up the economic scale than he could see himself ever going. The sofas were immense and lush, the carpet a thick weave, and the paintings on the walls had the telltale sculptural gleam of oil on canvas. He settled down near the edge of one of the sofas, his—all too light—suitcase beside it. Something was wrong, all his instincts were screaming it, but he couldn't put a finger on what it was. He had a pretty well-honed sense for danger, and he didn't think that was what was setting his alarms blaring. But still, something had unsettled him from the moment he'd walked in the door.

A clock was ticking somewhere in the vastness of Elly Pryce's house. Nick drummed his fingers on the side of the sofa as he listened to Elly bustling in the kitchen, humming a tune. Then he heard a familiar voice say his name—"Mr. Kurosawa"—and he knew all at once why his heart had been in his throat.

*

Umber stood in the doorway, dressed in a dark suit. He looked immaculately put together, and tired and in pain, all at once. So familiar to Nick's eyes, and behind a wall of anger and confusion there came a tide of helpless love. *I knew he was here. It's like I fucking smelled him.*

"Mr. Umber. I thought—I guess—" Nick laughed hoarsely. "I guess Miss Pryce had an ulterior motive after all."

"I hope you will not blame her," he said mildly.

"You..." Nick swallowed. "You left. You were gone. Didn't want me dragged in any further."

"I know. I know. Oh, Nick, I'm so sorry." His words were soft, but he remained still and bolt upright, hands grasping like claws over the handle of his cane. "You have no reason to trust me anymore. Say the word, and I will leave at once. You'll never have to see me again. I only—I only hope you do not hold it against Miss Pryce that she agreed to help an old acquaintance. She could use a good personal assistant. That much is true."

Nick laughed, a harsh and jagged sound. "And she'd send, what, updates to you on how I'm doing? Like a pet you gave up for adoption?"

"Nick—"

"You abandoned me." The words fell like lead slabs between them. "You can't just...show up, can't just undo that."

"I know. I know that!" His voice broke, just a little, and Nick could suddenly see through the cracks in his armor. Whatever his reasons, leaving Nick had, at least, not been easy for him. "And if I'd had the strength of my convictions, I wouldn't even try."

"You'd really leave right now, if I asked you?"

Umber swallowed and looked away. There was a slight tremor in his hands—so slight that most likely nobody but Nick would be able to see it. Nobody who wasn't attuned to Umber's every move, every minute expression. Nick fought with the urge to close his own hand over Umber's, to still that trembling. "I would."

"After going through all this trouble to...what? Get one more look at me?"

Umber froze, his hands white-knuckled on his cane, and Nick felt a moment of bitter triumph at even that slight sign of getting a rise out of him. It wasn't what he wanted, not really—but he wanted more than cracks in the armor. He wanted to see something real.

"Why did you leave?"

"You know why." Umber shook his head helplessly. "I didn't lie to you. It's fine for a man alone to live the way I do, always looking behind him, always ready to upend his life at the slightest notice. It's not what I wanted for you."

"It wasn't your choice to make." Nick had thought the words would come out angry, but instead his voice was strangely gentle—as if he were speaking to some wild thing that might flee.

"Well." He made a sound that could have been a laugh and walked with clumsy steps over to the nearest sofa, where he sat down with a hard thump that made Nick wince slightly. "I made the choice, in any case. And you're right—I can't just unmake it. But—"

A heavy warmth filled Nick's throat, his heart beating like a fist clenching and unclenching in his chest. He wanted to stand up, to go toward Umber, but something held him back, as sure as a leash.

Umber buried his face in his hands and laughed, a soft and desperate sound. "You told me I could use you, going on the run. That things were easier for me when I had to do it before. And you were right—you can tell that just by looking at me."

"Mr. Umber—"

He made a sharp, shaky gesture, cutting off Nick's words. His eyes were dark and hollow, their sea-glass shine muted. "That's not what I wanted you for. That's not why I had Elly call you. I need you to know that, if you know nothing else."

"I know that," Nick said softly.

Umber blinked, as if he'd expected Nick to argue with him.

"You could have had me with you. I wanted to be with you." Nick took a breath. "You fucked up, Mr. Umber."

Umber hesitated a moment, and Nick held his breath. Then, Umber's mouth quirked in a little grin. "I fucked up," he said.

That admission snapped the invisible leash. Nick rose from the sofa—as if in mirror image, Umber rose as well, awkwardly scrambling to his feet, one hand clutching his cane. He looked at Nick with something like defiance, or the semblance of it, but could not stop a grimace—of pain? Of sorrow?

"I fucked up," he said again, this time almost snapping it. "You deserve better."

"Damn right I do," Nick said.

It threw Umber off balance again, as if he'd expected something different, but he held Nick's gaze. "You don't want to spend your life tied to me. I'm one complication on top of another."

"And I'm simple, is that what you're saying?"

"No! I just—" He shook his head. "I wanted to protect you, Nick. From being entangled in…all this." He made a sweeping gesture that seemed to encompass himself, the two of them, the room—the whole world beyond it. "I went about it in the wrong way, to be sure, but I care for you too much to be as selfish as I wish to be."

"It's pretty fucking selfish to think you always know best."

Umber opened his mouth, closed it again. He cocked his head. "Maybe on this one subject, I have slightly more experience than you."

"Maybe so." There was no burn in Umber's voice, no real threat—Nick weathered his words without blinking. Something in him knew exactly what this was: a last token defense.

Umber took a halting step forward. The hand at his side made and unmade a trembling fist. "You should leave, Nick," he said. "You should—" He half laughed. "You should tell me to leave. Take Elly's offer."

"Mr. Umber..."

He turned away from Nick. "It would probably be the wise thing to do."

"Mr. Umber." Now Nick took a step forward, and then another. "You're an idiot."

Then he went to his knees.

It said everything that words would be too clumsy for. It said I forgive you. It said I am choosing you. It said let me belong to you.

Umber made an incoherent sound. He slid down beside him and took Nick's face in trembling hands. "I don't deserve this," he said, holding onto Nick, his mouth yearning toward him.

"Probably not," Nick agreed, and they both laughed. Then, they kissed.

The kiss lasted a long while. Nick realized, somewhere in the buzzing blankness of his thoughts, how rare their kisses had been. How rare, and how precious for it. The softness and heat was like coming home—and Nick on his knees, that was home as well. Whether Umber wanted to stand above him, or sit beside him. He leaned his head onto Umber's shoulder and let out a long, shuddering breath. Some weight he had been carrying since waking up, cold and alone in a motel on the outskirts of Westerley, had finally dropped away.

"I love you, you know," Umber said after a while, his voice barely more than a whisper.

"I know," Nick said, and found that he had known it, all along. "I love you too."

"And I'm selfish enough to get you in trouble for it. I just—want you too much."

Nick took his hand and kissed it, first on the knuckles, then in the hollow of his open palm. "You're allowed to want, Jacob Umber. Someone I love once told me that."

"I've had to leave Jacob Umber behind," he said, his smile a little crooked. "I've got a few new names, now."

"I figured." Nick still held his hand. "It doesn't matter what you're called. As long as we're together. As long as I'm yours."

"I think I will always want to be Umber, to you." He stood up slowly, leaning on Nick's shoulder, tangling a hand in his hair. Nick closed his eyes, shivering under his touch. *Home, I'm home.* "Whatever other names I might collect, that one is for you. I like the way you say it."

Umber bent down to kiss him again. When they parted, Nick was breathless with want, with happiness—breathless, and yet calm. He was exactly where he was supposed to be.

"Now what?" he asked, and half a second later added, "Mr. Umber."

"Well." The smile on Umber's face made Nick's stomach flip. "I rather think that's up to both of us, now."

Epilogue

It was three AM, and Siobhan Marks's flight home had been delayed for five hours now. The night outside was flat-black and clouded, like a dusty blanket. The airport lights made everything seem slightly to the left of reality, as if time itself just kind of gave up once it passed security.

After Jacob Umber had slipped away from her in Westerley, Siobhan Marks had wanted nothing more than to tell her superiors to shove the case up their collective asses. She'd been under-resourced and overworked for months on what was now known as the "Umber case" when it had broken open in the most unpredictable way. It wasn't any wonder someone as clever and resourceful as Umber—someone who'd dodged the authorities for decades—hadn't been nailed down by one sleep-deprived agent without so much as a field office within a hundred-mile radius. That hadn't been a realistic option, though, not if she'd wanted to keep her job. Instead, she had to listen and nod her head and say "yes, sir" when they not-so-subtly implied that if it weren't for her, Jacob Umber would be behind bars already, and then get back to work on her caseload.

Then, when Nick Kurosawa dropped off the grid, they'd sent her to chase him down. She'd recommended a higher level of surveillance on him previously and had been shot down; apparently, the resources were better allocated elsewhere. Well, she could at least grimly enjoy the dubious pleasure of "I told you so."

Quizzing Nick Kurosawa's few friends in Westerley led her to Elly Pryce. Butter-wouldn't-melt-in-her-mouth Elly Pryce, who'd nodded and said of course she'd met Mr. Kurosawa, interviewed him for a job in fact, too bad he hadn't quite been the right fit. He'd declined her offer to take a guest room for the evening and a morning cab back to the airport, and she hadn't seen him since.

Everything she'd said had checked out, but there had been something, some coruscating mischief about her, that twanged at Siobhan's senses. There was nothing she could hang her suspicion on, and "mischievous eyes" wasn't exactly cause for a warrant. Still, her tenuous connection to Kurosawa—and Jacob Umber, through him—was enough that at least a cursory look at Pryce's finances was okayed by her superiors. She'd come out squeaky clean...except that she'd paid for Nick Kurosawa's plane ticket. She'd had an explanation for that too. "I can afford to be selective, Agent Marks," she'd said, not smiling but with the same sparkle in her eyes.

"And you have no idea where he went after that?"

She'd given an elegant shrug. "If he didn't go back home, then I'm at a loss." After that, she'd smiled again, lighting up her narrow, actressy face. "I'm sorry I couldn't be more helpful, Agent Marks. I'd hate to think that's two people in a row who flew out to see me for nothing."

Siobhan had kept stony-faced. There was something very likable about Elly Pryce, but then, she'd liked Nick Kurosawa, as well, and look where that ended up. Maybe being an FBI agent just wasn't compatible with having interesting friends. Or interesting girlfriends.

Now, she was waiting for her flight home, idly reading the same page of her magazine ten times over before finally putting it down with a sigh. If they'd have given her more personnel, more authority, maybe Nick Kurosawa wouldn't be a dead end—maybe she could track him down and figure out what he knew. Unfortunately, failure seemed to be a self-reinforcing loop; if anything, they'd give her even less to do her job.

That he knew more than he'd let on, she was sure about, especially once she'd looked deeper into the facade that Jacob Umber had built—if you could call the life that he'd lived for the last decade a facade, at least. Siobhan had dug up every business transaction, every quote in the local papers, every social contact that she could. The last had been few and far between. Everyone had spoken of a quiet, principled man, someone who hated to show weakness as much as he loved to show generosity. He had been remarkably generous to Westerley (with stolen money, she'd reminded herself). If he'd been louder about it, there'd be a few kindergartens and homeless shelters with his name on a plaque.

The one thing that seemed harder to find was pictures. She'd never actually managed to meet the man, and somehow, he'd contrived to never let himself be photographed. Oh, there were surveillance videos of him—she'd gotten them from the tower block where he'd lived—but somehow, he always seemed to be wearing a hat, or turned away from the camera. His paranoia had served him well. She'd managed to put together a composite sketch, but those, she knew, were no substitute for a photograph.

Well, maybe in a few years she'd get another lead. Her mouth twisted. This case had been a time-sink, chasing down a thief half of whose victims didn't exist anymore, the corporations he had stolen from bought out or dissolved long ago. She wasn't naive enough to believe that every case she worked on would have some kind of world-shattering importance, but maybe she was naive enough—idealistic enough, maybe—to want to actually chase down the bad guys. Whatever Jacob Umber was, whatever his motives might have been, she couldn't quite believe that he was a threat to national security. Or to anyone's security. He might not have been Robin Hood exactly, but he sure as hell wasn't the Sheriff of Nottingham.

She smiled sourly. *No, that would be me.* She slouched heavily in the uncomfortable airport-lounge chair (would have been nice if she'd been expensed into the VIP lounge, at least) and leaned her head back, suppressing a groan. What she really wanted right now, more than anything, was to sleep. Hopefully her flight would get underway soon, and she could at least catch some shut-eye on the way back to the East Coast.

An announcement came over the airport speakers. Siobhan perked up a moment, but it wasn't for her flight. Vienna, she thought she'd heard, or Venice; some other lucky bastards getting to go home. She stayed slumped in her seat, head half lolling—from the corner of her eye she caught a sudden movement through the lounge, and focused on its source. Two men, one pushing the other in an airport wheelchair. The man in the chair had a shaved head and a neatly trimmed beard, and wore thick horn-rimmed glasses. The younger man pushing him had a shock of green hair, a curled mustache, and wore a leather jacket jingling with buttons and chains. Her lip twitched in a slight smile at the sight they made—then a soft little alarm bell went off in her head.

She followed their movement with her eyes, not wanting to give away that she was watching them. It couldn't be—what were the odds? She'd never met Jacob Umber before, and he'd certainly never been described as a bald man with a beard, but she had met Nick Kurosawa. He'd been clean-cut with a slight ragged edge to him, not...well, not a mustached rocker with green hair. How would anyone describe these two if they were asked? The guy in the wheelchair had a beard, and the guy pushing him had green hair, a mustache, and a leather jacket. Squinting, she mentally shaved off the hipster mustache, ditched the jangling leather, dyed the hair black. If this guy actually did that, wherever his flight would land, he'd instantly look like a different person.

He'd look like Nick Kurosawa. To a tee.

Her throat was dry. She could get up—she could run and catch up to them. Arrest them, right then and there. Or at least question them. She supposed there were other couples who'd look a bit like Nick Kurosawa and an older man. Not that many, but a few.

The speaker crackled again—her flight home was about to board. A ragged but sincere cheer went up from the sleepy-eyed denizens of the lounge.

She swallowed, and the dryness in her throat eased. The green-haired man and his companion in the wheelchair vanished down the corridor, probably to catch their flight to Vienna or Venice. She sat up and rolled her shoulders, cracking her neck. She could chase them, sure. She could spend a night in the local field office interrogating two men who may or may not be Nick Kurosawa and Jacob Umber. Or she could decide she'd been chasing shadows and go home.

They would be caught, sooner or later—she figured that much was inevitable. Men like the two of them didn't easily slip away into the night, no matter how far they went.

But, she decided, with a slight smile, it probably wouldn't be today.

About the Author

John Tristan is a multinational gay nerd, currently living in Manchester, UK. When he's not writing, he works in the voluntary sector; when he's not doing either, he's probably playing video games or tabletop RPGs. After his mother banned books at the table during mealtimes, he read the backs of sauce bottles. His stories are sometimes romantic, sometimes erotic, often speculative, and always queer.

Email: john@johntristan.com

Twitter: @johntwitstan

Website: www.johntristan.com

Also Available from NineStar Press

Connect with NineStar Press

www.ninestarpress.com

www.facebook.com/ninestarpress

www.facebook.com/groups/NineStarNiche

www.twitter.com/ninestarpress

www.ingramcontent.com/pod-product-compliance
Lightning Source LLC
Chambersburg PA
CBHW020328110726
47898CB00003B/783